MONA

MONA

Pola Oloixarac

TRANSLATED FROM THE SPANISH
BY ADAM MORRIS

FARRAR, STRAUS AND GIROUX

NEW YORK

Farrar, Straus and Giroux
120 Broadway, New York 10271

Printed in the United States of America
Originally published in Spanish in 2019
by Literatura Random House, Argentina
English translation published by Farrar, Straus and Giroux
First American edition, 2021

Library of Congress Cataloging-in-Publication Data
Names: Oloixarac, Pola, author. | Morris, Adam J., translator.
Title: Mona / Pola Oloixarac ; translated from the Spanish by
    Adam Morris.
Other titles: Mona. English
Description: First American edition. | New York : Farrar,
    Straus and Giroux, 2021. | Originally published in Spanish
    in 2019 by Literatura Random House, Argentina.
Identifiers: LCCN 2020043857 | ISBN 9780374211899
    (hardcover)
Classification: LCC PQ7798.425.L65 M6513 2021 |
    DDC 863/.7—dc23
LC record available at https://lccn.loc.gov/2020043857

Designed by Gretchen Achilles

Our books may be purchased in bulk for promotional,
educational, or business use. Please contact your local bookseller
or the Macmillan Corporate and Premium Sales Department
at 1-800-221-7945, extension 5442, or by email
at MacmillanSpecialMarkets@macmillan.com.

www.fsgbooks.com
www.twitter.com/fsgbooks • www.facebook.com/fsgbooks

1   3   5   7   9   10   8   6   4   2

For Asia

Mnemosyne, one must admit, has shown herself to be a very careless girl.

—VLADIMIR NABOKOV, *Speak, Memory*

MONA

1.

Come thirsty, and bring an appetite for Nordic delicatessen!"

This was the last line of the invitation she'd found in her campus mailbox. The Meeting was scheduled to start on Thursday, but writers traveling from abroad were supposed to arrive the day before. Sweden's biggest newspaper was organizing a special reception in conjunction with the local chapter of PEN. The occasion for these festivities was the presentation of the Basske-Wortz Prize, the most important literary award in Europe and one of the most prestigious in the world. The dress code for the event was something they called "smart casual," which probably meant the men were supposed to wear a blazer.

Mona calmly advanced through the crowd at the airport. Behind her sunglasses she wavered between substances, having drowned the pasty residue of Valium on her parched tongue with hot black coffee. Half a pill to cross the United States, another half to cross the Atlantic, and a tiny bit more for the connection from Paris to Stockholm. In California it was impossible to get her hands on any Valium—not unless she went all the way to Tijuana. So her shrink sent regular shipments from Lima. A side effect of the drug was that it seemed to slow her movements—something she thought made her look more elegant.

Can we talk?

Mona wore a beige raincoat, black leggings, and white sneakers. She was relatively tall. Strands of smooth brown hair cascaded from one side of a loose bun. Nobody could have mistaken her for a lawyer or a businesswoman—nothing in her appearance projected that degree of formality. And despite her serious demeanor there was something about her that was just a little off. The only visible trait that identified her as a writer was, perhaps, her terrible eyesight. Mona's prescription sunglasses were always filthy, but she was so farsighted that she never noticed. She removed them and squinted: her flight was on time, ten minutes until boarding.

Are you at home?

Unanswered texts accumulated on her phone, buzzing like a wasp in her pocket. Anyone watching might have seen her glance over her shoulder several times, as though she suspected someone might be following her.

You can't just run off like that. I'm coming over.

Boarding began, organized by flyer status. A few minutes later, Mona was in her seat. She loved flying. As the fuselage rose, her thoughts were free to roam the spongy terrain of clouds. She liked the feeling of being trapped in an ocean of air, unreachable, left to her own electronic devices,

4

imprisoned and free at the same time. Takeoff elevated her to a spiritual plane. She couldn't resist the impulse to say a few Ave Marias: memories of her days as a Catholic schoolgirl suffused her brain like a third drug. (In Lima, all the girls dressed in navy blue. They'd thrown her out of that school, too. Called it a medical leave.) Mona closed her eyes and imagined the aircraft rattled by a hurricane, then descending into the depths, dissolving into the blue immensity before finally exploding underwater. She'd simply cease to exist, with the incomplete masterpiece follow-up to her debut novel marooned on the laptop that would perish alongside her in the icy void. She found the idea relaxing.

Mona slumped back into her seat and massaged her neck. Her nearest neighbor was across the aisle. He resembled a giant toad.

You can't escape. We need to talk.

Was she escaping? she wondered, smiling to herself as she cracked the seal on a miniature bottle of Stoli. Entering through her earphones, Mina's "Malatia" (*Il Capolavoro Collection: Second Part*) coursed through her body, the sound disseminating like an additional narcotic. Her phone was calm now, a sleeping animal. Even if a few messages continued buzzing in her head, the switch to airplane mode had begun to have its soothing effect.

One explanation, she reasoned, was that madness had overtaken her. But it wasn't such a clear-cut case. Her sensei, the chair of the Department of Romance and Ibero-American Literatures, knew exactly where she'd gone. And she was still in touch with her students. Or at least with Raoul, her favorite, who'd written to find out how she was doing. He told her that her behavior—a professor who considered her a threat had called it her "disappearance"—was considered inexplicable. She knew her sensei had written her, too. But she'd given up on her Stanford inbox, which was filling with reminders of her obligations as a foreigner in the United States. Instead she set it to auto-reply: *I won't be reading emails for a while.* Not reading emails, in the heart of Silicon Valley, was tantamount to declaring oneself dead. The truth—or, rather, what she told herself at the time was the truth—was that she'd started writing one of those terrifying, brilliant, and dangerous books: a mantis lying in wait for its prey, half camouflaged by its own beauty, poised to attack. And now the book was starting to eat her alive.

Mona had arrived at Stanford not long after the waves she made with her debut novel tossed her onto the beach of a certain impetuous prestige—and at a time when being a "woman of color," in the vade mecum of American racism, began to confer a chic sort of cultural capital. American universities shared certain essential values with historic zoos, where diversity was a mark of attraction and distinction. By playing the part of an overeducated Latina adrift in Trump's America, Mona experienced academic captivity as a sort of serene freedom.

North American universities asked all doctoral candidates, upon application, to reveal their "ethnicity." Mona had clicked "Hispanic, Indigenous" and typed "Inca" in the box underneath. This was Silicon Valley, right? She might as well try to Lean In. Anchoring her identity to a brutal and exquisite empire about which so little was known would provide her with an ideal costume for the university's tribal masquerade. She'd been born in Peru, but claiming indigenous ancestry in any other context would've been outrageous—much like calling herself a "person of color" anytime prior to her arrival in the United States. There was a niche sort of glamour to it, like being a rare specimen of an endangered species—as though her mysterious DNA were a tiara encrusted with rare pearls, and the universities each a massive ark navigating the Great Flood of the United States, heroically fulfilling their mission to save two of each beast. Strictly speaking, Mona preferred to think of herself as more of a mermaid, that cross between the fantastic and the inexplicable whose true habitat was beneath the waterline, among the drowned. She couldn't help feeling like an outside observer, a mermaid tourist. Anyway, the whole charade was just a bizarre exercise in academic bureaucracy. And besides that, the selection of a racial subtype for "Hispanic" was obligatory.

Mona's identitarian fantasy was quite well received on campus (it related to her research topic) and offered her the opportunity to advance her career merely by being herself—as much herself as humanly possible. Later she realized it would have been even more advantageous to add on some kind of physical disability—a slight but evident defect—but nobody's perfect.

Even so, Mona enjoyed a unique advantage on campus:

her intellectual pedigree was well established by the time she arrived. The august critic Jorge Rufini had called her debut novel a "radical phenomenon" in a Cuban cultural journal of distinction: the literary Chanel of the Latin American left. The journal retained an indelible sophistication for having been founded by Fidel Castro as a cultural arm of the Cuban Revolution. Mona liked to imagine the back issues stacking up in the leader's bathroom. What Rufini liked about her novel—what he called its "vital commitment"—was its marriage of politics and literature, the *sancta sanctorum* of the Latin American Boom. Such a commitment, Rufini complained, had become "painfully rare" in her generation. This was an implicit snub of what other critics were calling "micropolitics" and "autofiction": two among the many intellectual currents that for Rufini (erstwhile editor of Julio Cortázar and beloved friend to many of the previous century's towering authors) were in fact so micro that they belonged to the category of literary microbes, sub-entities to which no one needed to pay the slightest attention. That was why Rufini offered his services as her Stanford sensei, catapulting Mona to the status of some kind of savior holding down the front lines of literature: the legitimate heiress to the Boom, a young tigress of that feral breed resulting from that marriage of guns and books, scioness of the only respectable aristocracy in Latin America.

There's no one else like you. Why are you hiding?

But at this exact moment, #rightnow in Mona's life, the principal subject wasn't so much the book she'd already written, but the one she couldn't finish writing—or, depending on the day, the utter falsity of her literary persona and the total lie she was living. "Just a bunch of shit to distract from the real problem, which is that she doesn't have any fucking idea how to tell a story." Someone said this about her on Facebook, in the comments under one of Rufini's posts about her novel. Reading it, Mona could feel the pixelated words burning into her heart even as she instinctively wrote them off, answering only by way of an ironic comment posted under one of her fake Facebook identities—the avatars through which the troll hemisphere of her brain found free expression.

I'm a part of your life. There's no denying it.

Mona's trolling profiles all had their own particular appetites, and some could become rather explosive in combination with her cannabinoid repertoire. The dom troll had a taste for White Recluse, a tetrahydrocannabinol of the highest voltage, engineered to hurl the user into an internal maelstrom, where she might better withstand the harsh realities of the year 2017. Mona took the advice of her chief troll and started vaping it daily. White Recluse was designed to obliterate every trace of paranoia, so a puff was enough to keep Mona's personalities split for six hours straight. She spent the time wrapped in a haze thick enough to get through classes and department events meant to facilitate "networking," a word Americans used to describe socializing with colleagues, as though they needed a concept to justify kindness and camaraderie at work.

What Mona enjoyed most about vaping was the furtive impunity. From far away, and even up close, it just looked like she was holding a pen. The wisp trailing from her mouth was hardly visible, and if anyone asked, she could say it was just apple flavoring. Mona could vape out in the open, for anyone to see—a behavior that had been definitively prohibited. Getting away with it only confirmed her suspicion that she was completely invisible. Nonexistent.

Mona usually saved her cyber hate rounds for nightfall in South America, when it was still afternoon in Palo Alto, where the California sun beat down upon the land without remorse. Eventually she'd power down her phone and fire up the vape, while in another dimension of collective consciousness—of which she certainly formed a part, and from which she'd never have the guts to escape—her digital self, now rendered defenseless, was thrashed and dragged. Mona nibbled the tip of her vape and hoisted herself back outside, shuffling her feet down the broad avenues, which in reality were street-level highways completely devoid of human life.

You know you can't just leave me like this.

Sometimes Mona ended up at the Palo Alto Caltrain station, where trains to San Francisco stopped. She'd sit on a bench and watch people get on and off the trains, stare at the empty tracks, and ruminate over the details of her possible demise: there she'd be, flat on her back as the travelers nudged her, checked for a pulse, patted her down, and searched her pockets for ID. They'd call Stanford, her beloved sensei, the academic secretary. And her body? Obviously the most logical thing was to donate it to science: the body of the deceased nonwhite Hispanic-Inca Latina of color would belong, of course, to the university. They wouldn't just cremate her—would they? Wouldn't that be a shame, a waste? What parameters would they use to distinguish her body from waste? If she were run over by a train, of course, it would totally destroy her lady parts. Of what use to science could she be in that case? And getting sawed in half under the Caltrain would be a breach of her university fellowship . . . No: it was better to remain a woman, Hispanic, South American, body intact, praise be to Saint Judith Fucking Butler. Mona imagined blond and Indian doctors in their white coats, stupefied by her luxurious but inert tits. Her thoughts segued into an elaborate postmortem orgy at Stanford Medical Center.

After the most recent of these episodes, a sordid sequence that unraveled into a total blackout, Mona had woken up on the platform. The California cannabis she consumed was top-notch.

When I close my eyes, I see you. With me.

She lifted a hand: her hair was stuck to the cement, her head a swamp. She didn't remember how she got there. Brain fog muddled the furniture, the bar. Light and dark shapes jumbled together, the avalanche after the earthquake. Her hands felt their way down her body: wet and cold. Something had happened, something horrible she couldn't remember. Her arm ached. She looked down to discover shredded, livid flesh. Her phone let out a hoarse whistle: it, too, was a survivor.

She went home and took a long shower, boiling hot, and hugged herself under the jets. She felt like she'd fallen several stories onto the pavement and absorbed the impact into her body. She stepped out of the shower and looked in the mirror: a violet blotch was spreading across her neck. Her face was intact, but her body looked like it had been rendered by Egon Schiele—or like a figure from one of Schiele's paintings who'd just crawled out of a car wreck. She didn't remember anything about a car, or having injected any Egon Schiele into her veins. She didn't remember a thing.

Maybe the pain was a pupa inside her, Mona thought: an amorphous substance awaiting the formation of a new exoskeleton. She recalled a viral video she'd seen hundreds of times, of a praying mantis slowly shedding its skin. If I go on like this, if I can go on like this—she said aloud—I might transform into something else. Alert to the sound of her voice, Mona's phone buzzed in reply. It was Google, suggesting that she check in for her flight. How could she have forgotten? The festival. Sweden. The Basske-Wortz Prize, for which she had been nominated.

Mona tied a silk handkerchief around her neck, covering the dark mark. She turned to gaze at her nude profile: at least she looked thin. And if she won the Basske-Wortz? She untied the silk handkerchief and arranged her things on the bed: European passport, wallet, several pairs of underwear (purple, black, green, and red), and enough decent

12

makeup to disguise her Egon Schiele deformities. How long did bruises last? She put on a black bra and pink panties, flounced onto the mattress, pulled her knees to her chest, and twirled her slender ankles, creating spirals with toenails painted in Chanel's Rouge Radical. Her left foot curved delicately toward the right, her toes lined up like a sinister family of faceless dwarves: *Our warmest congratulations*, Miss Mona Tarrile-Byrne. *The world is yours.*

2.

Two hundred thousand euros, thirteen finalists, one winner. Hailing from all four corners of the earth, the finalists convened for the Great Meeting: Sweden's most prestigious literary festival, held to commemorate the legacy of Edmond Virgil Basske-Wortz, Alfred Nobel's best friend. And if she won? She'd ditch Stanford for good and make straight for the jungle, penetrating deep into the forest until she lost herself in the wetlands of the Brazilian Pantanal. *If you moved to the Pantanal, you could survive on a hundred dollars a year and then use the rest of the money treating all the infections and diseases you'd contract. You could easily spend the remainder of your life in the jungle—because you wouldn't last long! Great idea!* Silenced on her phone, Antonio's voice prattled on in her head. Airplane mode was ideal for guys like him, the ones who felt the need to comment incessantly on her life.

She unbuckled her seat belt, unclasped the gold pillbox where she kept her mints, and sucked on another sliver of Valium. On the other side of the aisle, toad-man was stealing furtive glances at the passing flight attendants. Beside him, a woman slept with her head lolling against his shoulder. Mona inserted her earbuds ("Addicted to Love," Ciccone Youth) and slid her phone, snakelike, to the front of her leggings, so that the little hole for the charger was perpendicular to her clit. She closed her eyes. Pleasurable sensations accompanied her shift into Spa Mindset as she visualized the Meeting and the little golden basket containing the Basske-Wortz Prize, on the other side of the rainbow.

Her daydream adopted the aesthetic of a traditional Nordic porno: men in the sauna, barely covered by their towels, watching as she got boned in a frenzy of ecstatic alcoholism and barbituric delight. She didn't derive pleasure from any of the specific actions performed by her partners: there wasn't really a sequence of actions to follow in the first place. Rather, it was the sensation of losing consciousness that Mona associated with pleasure. She saw herself emerging from the sauna, on the brink of fainting and having lost nearly all muscular control, wrapped in a cotton robe that opened to reveal her leg, kissed and caressed by her first (and then a second, and a third) new cock-friend. As a native of Lima, she used to call them *pililas*, but after her first Argentine boyfriend, she'd started using the Argentine slang *pija*. Dicks were radars of attention, erotic antennae made for detecting every contour of desire in their surroundings. Lustrous and pink, the burning regions of her lusty, addicted chola body opened up. Toad-man was watching, wise to the scene. Mona didn't care. She wasn't into toadies, but it didn't matter. She could perfectly well empathize with the sexual desire she awakened in others, toad-men included: she found herself arousing, too. If there was no reason to separate them, she reasoned, then points of view could overlap, hysteria and sexual excitement blending together. Mona was so stoned that she popped an upper to counteract the pleasure-induced torpor. As if the festival were a suitable occasion for the best pretend party of her life, she was completely fucked up by the time she deplaned in Stockholm with her smart little carry-on.

The enchantment of arriving in the Stockholm airport for the first time offered Mona sufficient consolation after someone slammed into her with a luggage cart (another bruise . . . how long do bruises remain on the body?), but back in Paris she'd barely been able to repress a pained cry when security confiscated a toiletry case full of little luxuries she bought during the connection at Charles de Gaulle. The security agent, possibly from Marseille, gave her an understanding look to acknowledge the loss (Chanel and Clarins!), as if to say, *Sorry, you know the rules*. Mona splayed her arms and cracked the vertebrae in her neck as she submitted to the palpitations of another agent, a blonde with her hair pulled into a ponytail. When the blonde detected something hard near her crotch—a modest but nevertheless visible protuberance in her leggings—Mona shrugged, pretending she didn't understand French, so that the agent would have to insert a hand into her pocket. The blonde's fingers moved toward her crotch as Mona gazed at the distant ceiling, *C'est mon argent, vous comprenez*, arms stretched into a crucifix. The agent gently caressed the trapped coins.

At arrivals in Stockholm, a stooped, gray man held a piece of cardboard displaying Mona's name. He introduced himself as Sturluson, "Like Snorri—only a bit younger." He smiled, managing to frown a bit at the same time, like a friendly Siberian dog. Touched by this kind welcome, Mona smiled and gave him a hug. Sturluson made excuses for his Spanish. It wasn't as good as it used to be: lately he'd devoted himself to the study of medieval Castilian, and his Spanish had never been the same—nor would it ever be—since he'd translated the *Quixote* to Swedish and, later, to Finnish.

These little tidbits of information were the antechamber through which one had to pass in preparation for the Meeting and the Basske-Wortz Prize. That people as erudite and excellent as the Swedish/Finnish translator of the *Quixote* would spend their time collecting guests from the airport was offered as proof that this festival was as literary as could be: a veritable labor of love, undertaken by a priesthood convened by the very gods of books and talent. It was all meant to make the guests feel they were at home and among friends, literati *comme il faut*. And Snorri, for one, seemed perfectly comfortable with the code of false modesty in force, citing his accomplishments in the form of apologies for slight deficiencies in his linguistic superpowers. He continued by excusing himself for failing to have mastered the subtleties of

Peruvian argot: he had only passing knowledge of Spanish from the colonies.

They were interrupted by the arrival of Philippe Laval, the latest sensation in French literature. He and Mona had been on the same flight from Paris, but Mona only now noticed his circular black Ray-Bans inscribed within the larger pale circle of his face. Philippe's nose reposed upon little pillows of pallid flesh; he smiled briefly, offering his incipient baldness in a little bow. A Breton, Mona surmised, desperately hoping she hadn't already reached the summit of the Meeting's sex appeal. The other writer in Snorri's charge, an Algerian, was flying in from Qatar and had gone ahead to baggage claim. They'd have to wait for him. They each stood beside their elegant carry-ons; Mona couldn't evade a hot burst of Philippe's breath.

When he arrived, Khalil Al-Azem pressed everyone's hands between his palms in a warm greeting. He wiped a handkerchief across his forehead, marveling at what a fantastic flight he'd had: a flight attendant had read one of his novels, recognized his name, and bumped him up to premium economy: two hundred TV channels, excellent service. The Qatari airline was the absolute best.

In the car, Mona started feeling nauseated and mentally calculated how quickly she'd be able to roll down the window and stick her head out to barf. Up front, Snorri and Khalil were engaged in an animated conversation about *The Thousand and One Nights*. Laval seemed to have fallen asleep behind his Ray-Bans. Mona lowered her window. Fresh air caressed her eyelids with restorative gentleness. It was air that had swept across ice—indigo iceberg effluvia—and she found herself imagining Sweden as a giant ice floe she could press her entire body against, as if it were her lover.

At the welcome party, the visiting writers were received by the Minister of Culture, a cordial skinny woman with short gelled hair, sharp eyewear, and the general systematic air of a Wall Street lesbian. She addressed them in English: "Writers from Russia, Armenia, Germany, Iran, Israel, Macedonia, Peru, Algeria, South Korea, Japan, Albania, Italy, France, and Colombia! We are delighted to have you here in Sweden and hope that you'll enjoy the Meeting, which will begin tomorrow morning. The Basske-Wortz Prize will be given to one of you at the close of four days of rich conversation. Although only one author will take home the two hundred thousand euros, the fact that each of you has been nominated—and that you are all now here with us—is a literary achievement of its own, as well as a special honor for the organizers of this Meeting." The minister then thanked everyone in Swedish, explaining that her English was "just for business," and that since their subject was literature—that labor of love—she would prefer to speak French, which happened to be her favorite language, as she loved French literature. She then proceeded to commit various acts of gory violence against French grammar and pronunciation. Mona amused herself by watching Philippe, who wore a tragic expression and appeared to be engaged in a careful study of the floor. The other guests descended upon the buffet while Mona, who still wasn't done with her bender, sipped a cool glass of cava. Since none of her clothes were visible underneath her raincoat, Mona's outfit made her look like a flasher. Sheltered behind her cava glass, she assessed the contingent of writers who would be her company for the next several days. But soon she tired of speculation, and she wasn't feeling particularly social. She Google Mapped her way back to the hotel.

Can we talk? I'll be on Skype.

Stockholm's streets were a blue, deserted maze. A coat of moisture covered the entire city, giving the cobblestones a cinematic luster. Mona's boots didn't have decent traction, causing her to slip repeatedly. The more she slid, the more she hurried. She clasped the key to her Palo Alto apartment as her phone continued buzzing, alerting her to the arrival of messages that would go unanswered. She felt faint at several points along the way.

You know what the worst part is? I'm worried about you, Mona.

Back in her hotel room, Mona stretched out on the firm, tightly made bed. She untied the handkerchief around her neck and touched her left shoulder, which burned and ached, as if the pain were migrating through her body. How long do bruises last? She turned on the bathroom light and switched off the others, leaving the room in shadows. She thought it might be nice to vomit, just to clean out her system, but she lacked the proper motivation. She rolled onto her stomach, puffed her vape, and sprawled across the length of the firm bed. The harsh glare of her computer screen illuminated her buttocks, two gently rolling hills. On Skype, an avatar tittered in green: incoming call.

Mi senti? Mi senti?

Mona peeled off the Band-Aid she kept over the camera—it was how she protected herself from potential spies, hackers, and literary enemies. She had thirty unread messages from Antonio, which she deleted immediately. He wasn't the one calling.

"Mona, *mi senti?*"

On-screen, greeting her shirtless in Italian, was Franco. He knew the language of Dante aroused her. Franco was the kind of Italian you could only find in the United States, or really anywhere outside Italy. Or, as Franco more succinctly put it: he was tall. The fundamental axis of his existence was to prove that, no, Italians aren't all warm, friendly, or sweet. Or maybe they are, but only when they're low to the ground and have even lower self-esteem. Like a cat, Franco moved with the sun, always finding the exact spot where his blond head would shine fluorescent in the light. He let his eyelids droop with a melancholic air, confident in his ability to conjure the image of vintage Marcello Mastroianni.

Mona licked her lips. She crossed and uncrossed her stockinged legs, a little detail that she thought Franco would like. She felt ravishing in a way that he couldn't fully appreciate, as she then confirmed by slipping her fingers underneath her silk panties. (Maybe more ravishing than usual, because she'd forgotten to bathe.) Franco and Antonio overlapped: it wasn't unusual for them both to be jiggling green on her screen at the same time. That, however, was all they had in common. The thought derailed her: Mona didn't want to think about Antonio. She'd banished him and anything having to do with him to total ostracism, perpetual airplane mode. As soon as she so much as sensed his presence—via one of his constant messages—she hit delete and mentally clicked *Empty Trash*. Franco, on the other hand, was much more appealing—and the Italian language drove her wild.

Mona met Franco during a semester in Princeton, where she was finishing a master's before switching coasts for Stanford. The department at Princeton fostered a certain camaraderie among the students by making sure wine, cheese, and cookies were always on hand at lectures, to lure famished graduate students into attendance. Life at American universities was hard, and especially so at Princeton. Far from their natural habitats, the Latin Americans there passed through periods of numbness. Frozen alive, they responded only to the monastic discipline demanded by the academy, which supplied their spartan shelter and stipends. Inside they burned with the memory of human contact, the feeling of what it was like to be among other people. Mona and Franco had exchanged fancy credentials before a lecture, then sized each other up at a few rows' distance. Franco slipped out of the room just before the talk started. Through the half-opened door, Mona watched him fill his backpack with cookies and leftover Gouda. During the lecture, titled

23

"The Late-Medieval Amazonian Culture: Perspectives and Omissions," she forgot about him completely. She was busy annotating references for an essay she was concocting about the part of the Amazon basin that remained hidden after the Conquest—a secret world that had resisted the arrival of Europe from within the impregnable darkness of the jungle. The Amazon fascinated her because there, anything that seemed real, sacred, and *existent*, dissolved . . . and Mona knew with visceral certainty that hiding within that slippery monstrosity was a world beyond time: the cave, the real and actual Platonic Cave that rendered every other theory of knowledge mere illusion. The only way of finding this cave in Western culture was first to leave that culture behind. The hidden Amazonic giant had a spirit of its own; it electrified her, assured her that everything was still possible, waiting to be done, hidden only for the time being, encoded in a lineage of texts *obscuri per obscuriam* that only her finger could trace. After the talk, Mona dispensed with the idea of assailing the presenter with questions, preferring instead to reorder her profuse notes. She crossed and uncrossed her long legs, sheathed in jeans. Having returned in time for the Q&A, Franco interpreted her behavior as a performance explicitly meant to communicate her desire to be alone with him. He invited her to a private party at a real speakeasy in town, operated by a Turkish woman who ran a bar and roulette table in her garage.

They split a cab to the Turkish woman's house, where Franco guided Mona across a back patio adorned with a woodpile and some overgrown grass. Mona followed him, delighted to place her trust in a tall, hip Italian. She'd never been to this part of town, a humble neighborhood full of simple homes.

They came to a porch streaked with mildew, where Franco spoke the password. Someone said, *Hey*, and the Turkish woman unlocked the door. They followed her through the kitchen, where two children, hunched over brown plates, watched them go by. In the dining room, a group of men played cards in silence. Mona and Franco arrived at an improvised bar with seats upholstered in a strident, flowery pattern.

They drew up to the corner of the bar and ordered two Glenlivets, neat. After the Turkish woman showed the way to the bathroom, Mona disappeared down a hallway and returned fresh, her black, sleek silk top over gray jeans cinched with a pleather belt to accentuate her waistline— and therefore, her booty. She was the only woman in the whole place—that is, aside from the proprietress, who periodically came and went from the kitchen with a tray, trading empty glasses for full ones. She was acting the part of self-sacrificing nanny to the guys playing blackjack in the dining room. As they sipped their Glens, Mona started telling Franco about her vision of Andean literature coming down the mountain like a violent rockslide. She told him about Runasimi, the language of the people—and how it was the talisman of a future literature, because it obliterated the rancid music of the world as they knew it (the white man's fake news). The whiskey loosened her tongue as well as her hands, which moved up and down, offering glimpses of her lavender bra. But Franco didn't seem to notice when her bra made its several appearances. His Mastroianni gaze floated in the distance, in the direction of the Turk's bathroom. He listened to Mona with a somewhat serious, academic expression until he stuck his tongue down her throat by way of counterargument.

On Skype, Franco was in nothing but boxers. He gazed at the camera as he slowly massaged his cock with delicate movements, as though it were a tubular little teddy bear. Mona arched her back like a cat, trying to fit her stockings in the frame behind her proffered ass. They'd met in English but usually spoke to one another in Spanish.

"I told you what Gabriela said to me, right?" (Franco smoothed his blond coif, a hypotenuse that angled down to the tip of his cock at the bottom of her screen.)

"No." (Mona shaped her mouth into a kiss.)

Franco's cock wavered in the air, annoyed.

"Really? I didn't tell you? She said that the field would never be the same . . . after my paper is published."

"She actually said that?"

"I already submitted it for MLA. I'm going to revolutionize the field with this paper. Seriously. *Vieni più vicino al cazzo.*"

Franco brought his dick closer to the camera and softly sang a verse from Cavalcanti (*Va tu, leggera e piana / dritt'a la donna mia*). Mona touched her pussy, focusing the frame on its triangular shape. She'd waxed a few days beforehand and her pores grazed the pink fabric of her panties like the wet snouts of tiny rabbits. Mona caressed herself until a cold blast overpowered her: Antonio's icon jumped (three new missed calls) and her mind went blank. Obeying her reflexes, she blocked him. Mona closed her eyes, trying to get back into the scene. When she reopened them, Franco was staring intently at something else on his screen, focused on something that wasn't her.

3.

During the first group outing, before piling into the van to the Meeting, they managed to lose track of the Armenian poet somewhere in downtown Stockholm. Did anyone remember what he looked like? Nobody seemed capable of recalling a single characteristic feature except for the fact that he was an Armenian poet. Maybe he had curly brown hair? But was he short or tall? What did he look like? "How should I know what he looks like? He looks like an Armenian poet!" yelled one of the Arab writers from the back of the van. Mona was sitting next to an older woman, a writer from South Korea, and trying to concentrate on the bilingual edition of Tranströmer she'd bought in the airport.

"So nobody's seen him? Nobody remembers speaking to him since we left the hotel?" Lowena, the assistant coordinator of the Meeting, persisted in her interrogation. As the editor of *Skogsrå*, a literary review based in Stockholm, she was one of the Meeting's infallible fixtures: she'd been on board since 1994, when the Meeting started as a camping retreat on the outskirts of Malmö. Now, she kept reminding them, the festival's prestige required four days of lectures and pleasant conversation at an exclusive resort in the Swedish countryside. Four days of intrigue and quiet desperation, until the winner of the Basske-Wortz Prize and its €200,000 booty was finally declared.

Outside the van, a line of ducks tottered genteelly through the plaza, paying no heed to the encroaching humans. They were fat birds, similar to swans but stouter, shocking in their total indifference to *Homo sapiens*. Leaning against a window, Mona felt an urge to get out of the van and follow them around, a little carpe diem and leg stretch while the search for the Armenian poet continued. The Korean lady sitting beside her had started knitting something in pastel wools. Trotting along after some ducks with a head full of Valium—what a splendid idea, Mona thought, before submerging once more in Tranströmer.

The blue sky's engine-drone is deafening.
We're living here on a shuddering work-site
where the ocean depths can suddenly open up

"Oh, Tranströmer," the Korean lady said, glancing at her sideways as she kept knitting. What did she think of him? Mona wanted to ask. What did Tranströmer remind her of? If she came across one of his poems, lost in the galaxy of poems whispered by the universe, would she be able to recognize it? Was the Tranströmerness of the world something visible? What did she think? But Mona couldn't move her mouth to form a single question. The Korean lady continued knitting impassively.

Trapped between her book, the Korean lady, and the window, Mona listened to the amiable murmur of conversations among the other writers. Everyday banalities: Oh, I didn't know that Karl Ove Knausgaard was invited to the last Meeting. Yeah, two years ago, actually. He's a pretty interesting guy. He used to bring his wife, Linda, but ever since they separated—that's the theme of his most recent novels—they divvied up the European literary festivals so they wouldn't have to run into each other. Modiano is a middle-brow author, but one of his books from the seventies, *Missing Person*, is amazingly cinematic. Is that a *good* thing now, in today's literature—being cinematic? This last question, croaked out by one of the men, was left hanging in the air.

The Armenian poet finally returned to the van. He'd been buying souvenirs for his kids and lost sight of the swarm of writers as they made their way across the city. He was athletic and short, with one of those tumultuous Marxist beards that were so popular in Brooklyn. The other writers applauded as he approached; the gigantic Russian gave him a drunkenly effusive hug.

"I'm glad to know we haven't contributed any further to the Armenian genocide," the Algerian writer quipped, generating a smattering of polite laughter.

Someone else remarked that it would've been great

publicity for this year's Basske-Wortz if the poet had vanished for good: prize ceremonies were an ideal and underutilized setting for a crime. The disappearance of a man from a small nation, a poet no less, would make for a difficult mystery to solve: What sort of enemies could such a man possibly have?

"It would only be difficult for a bad writer," a woman remarked dryly, her stern gaze barely making it over the rim of her glasses.

"Armenian poetry is not dead!" someone shouted from the back of the van, in an indeterminate accent.

The loss and subsequent recovery of the Armenian poet produced a passing euphoria. As though spurred by this sudden energy, the driver revved the engine.

They drove two hours north, toward the Arctic. The van and its precious cargo of writers cut across a series of blue and green panoramas, succeeded by conifers, meadows, and rocky formations in cream and pinkish brown—like marbled cascades of ladyfingers. The sky took on the metallic hues of a lightning storm gathering in the distance. They still hadn't seen much of that Swedish summer sun the Minister of Culture had promised them. Lowena, sitting beside the driver, predicted they'd have beautiful weather over the weekend. But just in case, they'd each received a yellow plastic poncho along with their Meeting program, as well as a notebook bearing the words "Writer's Block," and a catalog containing each of their photos, printed in color.

Mona slept almost the whole way, hugging the catalog and her volume of Tranströmer as if they were her favorite pillows. When they stopped to get out of the van, she put her dark glasses back on. Still half asleep, she slinked off to her cabin, a gabled cottage divided into two apartments. Symmetrical twin benches were stationed on the porch like mute guards. Mona climbed the stairs, suitcase in hand. She tumbled into the cabin and landed in bed, a profound sense of pleasure emerging from somewhere deep within her Herculean hangover.

Half an hour later, a man in a gray overcoat climbed the same stairs to enter the contiguous cabin. He was an Icelandic poet, with the long beard of a dervish. Dragging a small carry-on behind him, he entered his room and locked the door behind him.

That night, Mona dreamed of a black body of water ascending from the lake, carrying with it a silent cargo of dead animals drowned by the tide. The dark liquid entered through the keyhole and took her by surprise in bed as it spread across the floor. The chair clattered against the desk, knocked into it by the current. The windows were open. Something was watching her from outside, panting. Better not to scream, she thought, or the hungry beast prowling around out there will come in and find me. She woke up shaking, drenched in sweat.

4.

The Meeting kicked off at 9:00 a.m. The program listed a series of panels, with breaks for coffee and lunch. On the last day, after they'd all given their lectures, the Basske-Wortz Prize would be awarded during a ceremony held at sunset by the lake (and if it rained, in the building they called Patrick Hus, where communal activities—such as breakfast, lunch, and dinner—would be held). The lectures would all take place in a spacious white tent pitched on a lawn at the top of a small hill. Part of the tent was occupied by a low wooden platform; the rest was filled with rows of wooden benches easily mistaken for church pews. Along one side, interpreters were seated in little booths, where they performed simultaneous translation for each of the speakers. The writers had been asked to send their talks ahead of time, in English, and each was now available in Swedish translation. Outside the tent, the horizon dissolved into the mirror-calm bay of a lake, and the hill softly descended into a meadow filled with little white and yellow flowers.

Mona entered slowly, a mug of green tea in hand. Aside from the jet lag, she'd slept too much, deep beneath thick layers of Ambien and Valium. She took a seat at the back of the tent, where it would be easier to slip out for a cigarette. Mona didn't usually indulge, but she considered herself a social smoker, particularly when socializing with other writers. They made her anxious—more so if she had to spend several days with them in an environment that allowed few avenues of escape. The only comforting thing about the Basske-Wortz Meeting was that there were so few "Spanish" writers there. Writers take their languages so seriously, to the point of aggression. The phony solidarity of having a "Latin" culture in common with other writers was something that always repulsed her. And socially—that is, in the global society of writers, the society to which she belonged, albeit in a forcefully reluctant and itinerant way—there was nothing worse than falling in with a bunch of déclassé monolinguals. Mona felt much more comfortable in the company of other languages. That is, she preferred to live *en traducción*, according to her literary tastes: she was much more interested in Japanese lyrics of terror and Nigerian poetry written in Hausa than she was in reading about rich narcos, rich intellectuals, and intellectuals who got rich writing about the poor in Miraflores, Buenos Aires, Mexico City, or Santiago—it was all so boring. Anyway, sharing a language could turn into a complicated chore, requiring translations much harder than Hausa to Spanish. Once, during the ceremony for a different prize (she didn't win), Mona was verbally assaulted by a writer from Murcia who misunderstood one of her jokes. The Spaniard had attempted to praise Peruvian literature by resorting to the commonplace courtesy of defenestrating the literary culture of his home country. Mona told him that she hadn't boarded two flights just to hear people say nice things about other Peruvian writers, and proceeded to launch her own defense of Peninsular literature: "Our Javier Cercas would wreck your Vargas Llosa in two seconds flat!" This gauntlet thrown, Mona figured he would pick up the joke and run with it, but her pique only sparked his Murcian rage, burning not merely at her words—he wasn't listening anyway—but at the confident and self-sufficient way that Mona had negotiated this public *côté*, transforming a leisurely exchange into something that seemed more like a real intellectual challenge—something that had become unusual at those types of events. The guy got up from the table, still wagging a finger at her, while Mona, seated between two men who had no idea what was happening, laconically replied that there must have been some kind of misunderstanding: Maybe he didn't understand her colonial Spanish? Life in translation, on the other hand, was like swimming in an Olympic pool: people could cheerfully ignore each other. Everyone adopted an Anglo-Saxon deference and stayed in their own lane. This allowed Mona to luxuriate in her own exoticism, gliding freely through her very own ocean, feeling special and unique.

But it wasn't just a linguistic preference. In general, European writers were already used to the idea that nobody cared about what they wrote. They were crystal-clear on the insignificance of their role in contemporary society, and it translated to humility in their conduct. But things weren't the same everywhere: in some cultures the writer still retained a rock-star status, and this esteem wasn't always salubrious. Philippe, the Frenchman, exuded an aura of unhappiness and a general reticence regarding any sort of participation in human life. It radiated from him like a magnetic field, throwing off a skein of dark energy. When he passed in front of Mona, he glanced back at her from the corner of his eye, Moleskine in hand, before taking a seat next to one of the side exits. Latin American writers liked to fantasize that they shared this French exceptionality. But this self-conception, Antonio had remarked during one of their first encounters, was merely based on the experience of white people raised in semiliterate countries. Mona's hand quivered, spilling tea across her notebook. Why did she tremble at the mere thought of Antonio? *Empty Trash*, she muttered.

She felt nauseous, numb, not entirely prepared to confront humanity; maybe the signal emanating from Philippe the Afflicted was afflicting her in turn (though, much as Mona tried to deny it, the affliction was Antonio's venom collecting in her brain, stinging like the tentacles of a jellyfish, hidden underwater). She remembered something she'd heard a while back from her friend Vlad, a sixty-something Russian novelist she'd met at Iowa during a prestigious writers' residency in the middle of Yankee Nowhere, at a time when Mona was still a newcomer to the circuit. According to Vlad, a self-declared expert on Nabokov's superiority over his Russian contemporaries, peace reigned in Iowa "only because we don't understand each other's languages, and our ignorance protects us." Vlad had a Tatar's slanted eyes and hailed from Georgia, the Soviet region most punished by Stalin, its famous native son. To illustrate his point, Vlad told Mona he'd participated in residencies that included composers and musicians as well as writers—and that was real hell. Peace between musicians, Vlad continued, was impossible, because they could all tell who was a real genius and who was just a mediocre poseur. Music was a transparent field in which genius and mediocrity were self-evident truths—and this only ever led to hatred, distrust, and malaise. No doubt about it: not knowing each other's languages was the key to conviviality, because if we were able to read what everyone else was writing, if we were able to understand it and feel it like music, the Russian calmly concluded, well, then we'd be murdering each other in our beds.

Mona balanced her notebook across her knees and sipped what remained of her tea. Something, someone, was observing her intently. She turned her head and smoothed her hair, casting a furtive gaze over her shoulder. She was startled to confront the black eyes of a fox, fixated on her. She'd never seen a fox in real life; it almost seemed a hallucination, pausing there at the tent's open flaps, handsome and tragic, with an otherworldly glow. Mona held out her palm so the fox could come over and sniff it. But the vixen disappeared, her caramel tail waving like a feathered fan.

A brunette woman sat down beside Mona, flapping a white shawl over her shoulders. She wore a close-fitting red dress, somewhat low-cut, and had stabbed her way across the lawn in red stilettos. She was probably about fifty. "How lovely," Mona whispered, more curious than admiring. Her entire look was an ode to the impractical, the incarnation of a certain sort of literary idea of what it means to be a woman. Her *belle poitrine* was easily discerned; she looked like she'd just walked out of a detective novel in which her destiny was to be murdered by a minor character (such as the unreliable witness). She met Mona's compliment with a broad smile.

"I never take off my heels. *Sono una donna italiana!*"

"*Brava!*" Mona replied. She hadn't realized there would be anyone from Italy at the Meeting. Oh, right, an author from Sicily, Fabrizzio Castelli or Castelloni—something like that. The woman introduced herself as Carmina. She was born in Albania and this was her first time in Sweden. Mona imagined Carmina winning the Basske-Wortz Prize and giving interviews from aboard a yacht, smiling in Dolce & Gabbana dresses, surrounded by impoverished children.

The speakers had taken their places at the front of the tent. The first, Abdollah Farid, brought his thick mustache close to the microphone. Wearing a blue blazer and glasses with orange designer frames, Abdollah was giving them a vague Omar Sharif vibe. His voice was dark and deep, and he pronounced his *v*'s and *w*'s like a German.

"My story begins in Iran, around the time I was getting

ready to leave the country. I was twenty years old when the revolution broke out, and the Iran that I'd known was about to disappear. I loved life, I loved liberty, and life as I'd known it in Tehran had ended for good. A man offered me a passport and safe passage to New York for fifteen thousand dollars. For nine thousand, I could go to Italy. I only had ten thousand, so the guy said he'd take me to Denmark and from there to New York. The first place we ended up was a refugee camp on the outskirts of Copenhagen. I won't say much about that part, though, because the day is just getting started and I don't want to be a downer. When they finally released us and let us go into the city, I barely had enough money to survive. I couldn't afford the trip to New York. So I stayed in Copenhagen."

Abdollah glanced up to observe his audience over the rims of his orange glasses, as though checking his listeners' vitals.

"Never in my life had I heard a single word in Danish. I had to learn it all from scratch. I got a small apartment, a friend of the family from back in Iran got me a job, and that was how I spent the next two years, during which I kept writing in Farsi. But I was an idiot, wasting time. I'd never make enough money to live in Denmark if I kept writing in Farsi. I realized I had to learn Danish fast, so that I could write in Danish. In those days my mustache was big and bushy and black, and there were plenty of Danish ladies ready to help me out. Beautiful Danish ladies. And they fell in love with me, and I wrote as best I could, and they corrected my terrible beginner's Danish. That's how I published my first book of stories in Danish."

Abdollah paused to take a sip of water.

"So that's how I became a success. I published six novels in Denmark, five books of stories, and most recently a translation of the Koran—which now, to my delight, is finally being translated into Swedish." He added this last part with a light inclination of his skull. "This was my gift to Europe: to bring this magnificent work of language and compassion to occupy the place it deserves—that of a classic work of distinguished prose. And people came to me and said, Abdollah, your books are published all over the place. You win prizes, you have money. You have a wonderful home, a beautiful wife, a TV. People read and discuss your work. Critics appreciate your books, and so do regular people. What more could you want? And I tell them, I want more! Denmark is a small country where they think that success is enough. But it's never enough!"

Laughter, stifled up to this point, rippled under the tent. Abdollah's egomaniacal candor was irresistible. There was something so direct and real about his happiness that put everyone at ease. Except for Carmina, she of the red stilettos: as Abdollah spoke, Carmina pulled the white shawl over the top of her head and coiled the loose end around her neck. It seemed to have spiraled into a hijab. She sat there listening gloomily, dead serious.

"What I'm about to tell you now is something I tell all

the young Arab men I meet, the young guys arriving here to Europe. I see them in the street and they look timid to me, awkward. They feel like they don't belong—you can see it in their faces, in their attitudes. They're not happy. They try to be like Europeans and it doesn't work, because they can never achieve that. They think they have to hide a part of themselves, to trade the Arab in them for the future European who's hiding inside, waiting to emerge. Substitute one for the other. And I tell them: No! You don't have to hide, and you don't have to assimilate. It's just the opposite. Precisely the opposite. It's your Arab customs, your Arab manners, that the Europeans have to learn and assimilate for themselves. Because . . . Europe is pregnant! Pregnant with our children! There are millions of us already living here, and millions more on the way. They can try to contain it for a while, but nobody, *nobody* will ever be able to stop it! And we're here to stay!"

Mona applauded, doubled over with laughter. Abdollah Farid was pulling a Kanye West, the Kanye of "BLKKK SKKKN HEAD," a fantastic King Kong avatar in total command of his charm and power. She couldn't help feeling delighted whenever someone exotic (as exotic as her) gave voice to the threat they represented, casting off the minority roleplay and the fake amiability to the dominant culture. Abdollah had come to pronounce an inevitable prophecy: Did you think the "Muslim problem" was just terrorism and women who refuse to wear bikinis and swim in pants? Think again.

The writers from Algeria and Armenia applauded rabidly,

infected by Abdollah's enthusiasm, while the Nordics smiled and made animated comments about his delivery. It was obvious that Abdollah had abandoned any illusion of winning the Basske-Wortz, and could therefore entertain himself by giving whatever kind of speech he wanted. Part of the euphoria unleashed in the audience had to do with the certainty of his loss, as if his valiant abdication had electrified them. His was an elegant solution: instead of waiting for the bomb to drop at the prize ceremony, Abdollah had decided to peacock around the Meeting and launch his own missiles. Mona amused herself by imagining Europe knocked up with millions of zygotes, the map of the continent appearing to her like a woman splayed out across the water, wearing Italy's boot on one foot, with an arm extended (waving for help? squirming with pleasure?) in the shape of Denmark. How could anyone convince the women of Europe that there'd be nothing in it for them as long as hot Middle Eastern guys kept turning up? A massive hit of DNA, bayonets of semen penetrating European uteruses in a sweeping paramilitary strategy, uncontainable because it was based on seduction and love— and love and seduction can't be corralled in refugee camps.

Mona noticed a very handsome man watching her as he applauded, entertained by the whole situation. He was too handsome to be a novelist; he had to be a journalist, or a nonfiction author. He was wearing a jacket with a high collar, made of lambskin or imitation-lambskin, similar to the one from *Blade Runner 2049*. He looked Nordic, but with dark hair. Perhaps he was an "Alpine," as Goebbels liked to call the darker Aryans. Mona massaged her neck and returned his smile. Maybe he was just another gringo.

But Abdollah's admonishing speech wasn't over:

"I've told you the story of how I became a Danish writer, but I omitted an important detail. The most important of all. I didn't tell you that I had an advantage. I already knew what it was like to create a language from scratch. To invent my very own language. My father, in Persia, was deaf-mute from birth. Ever since I was little, the only way he could communicate with me was through the signs we invented. We had our own language, my father and I. A language is always an invention of the world from scratch, even if it's just between a father and son. Learning a language means inventing every single thing it might contain, even though it usually seems like language is something that already exists, something that was already here before us, if only because other mouths have already pronounced the words. I started to write stories from a young age because I felt I had to give voice to my father, who died without having ever been able to hear his own voice. I had to give voice to the people of my city. I had to give voice to the people of Iran. That's why I write, even today: to give voice to those who have only known silence."

Mona had stopped laughing, like everyone else in the tent. Her mind had been transported to a noisy, yellowed street from a Naipaul novel, where Abdollah's deaf-mute father wandered with his big, honey-colored eyes full of things he could never express. The patience of the child, their silent love . . . Abdollah had transmitted all this without explicitly

45

mentioning it. He'd lifted and wrenched their hearts using only the power of his voice. Mona's thoughts turned to those guttural, prehistoric nights of the human species, when everything was made of stars and cawing birds: everyone went out to hunt, strong women and men dragging themselves across the earth, invisible to the beasts. Those who couldn't hunt remained behind, the ones who couldn't leap in front of a mammoth or throw a spear, the old and the young and the crippled: this was how language had emerged, because it was cold and dark and they could barely see. So they had to communicate aloud, rather than gesturing—but in whispers, lest they be devoured.

How many things remained buried in silence? The extant universe had conjured itself ab ovo, from scratch, and with the force necessary to penetrate the crushing avalanche of erasure, so that the history of *what really happened* wouldn't remain trapped and invisible beneath. Silenced. She trembled despite herself.

Mona removed a mentholated Kleenex from her bag: a little tear had formed under her eye. Sometimes she was overcome by emotion, sudden seizures amid the internal storms that she repressed as best she could. A tiny tear could suddenly become a cascade, like one of those shamanic transformations in which a man swims across a river and emerges as a puma on the other side—only that Mona carried the river and the pumas and everything else she didn't want to encounter on the inside, ready to burst. She was brimming with tension, to the point of overflow. Huffing the menthol from a Kleenex in her clenched fist helped Mona retake control of her facial muscles and regain her international poise.

"I'm crying, too," a masculine voice whispered from behind. Mona turned around. The man's green eyes were resplendent, dewy beneath the soft vapor rising in the sunlight filtering through the white tent.

It was Chrystos, a young author from Macedonia who'd exchanged timid glances with her at the PEN party. He had radiant white skin and delicate pink lips. Mona had looked him up in the Meeting program after the party and was delighted to learn that he self-identified as a fairy. She discreetly handed him her pack of Kleenex. Sharing a gentle cry with a fairy: Wasn't it unthinkable, and therefore adorable? She was delighted she'd come to the Meeting now. Maybe it wouldn't be necessary to drink her way through it—at least not all of it. Maybe it would be possible to go a few days without being completely intoxicated. Maybe, after this interval of intrigue and anguish, she'd emerge triumphant, crowned and draped in the delicious ermine cape of the Basske-Wortz Prize and attended by its retinue of euros. Maybe she'd only be truly lost if she were somewhere else instead. Mona recalled a writer she'd met during a residency in Provence: a woman from Hawaii, the author of a book that had been adapted to film, who told her she never read anything in translation. "America is so big, there's already so much to read!" the Hawaiian writer explained. She said there was a Nebraskan literature and a Northern Californian literature and Southern Gothic literature, and then of course there was the emerging Hawaiian literature, to which her work was foundational. Writers were figuring out the local stories that their target markets wanted to consume. And as offerings diversified, they cultivated new readers, such that eventually every local writer would supply his readers with stories, and these local writers would be able to live off what they wrote, just like a berry farmer who sells organic red currants at the farmers market on Saturdays. They were riding in a French sculptor's Peugeot 308, crossing vineyards en route to the Marquis de Sade's estate. It was a curvy road, and the Hawaiian asked the sculptor to slow down because she was feeling carsick. After a silence, Mona told her, "Well, I could have stayed home, too, and never learned English or French. But it's more fun to be out in the world, to get to know it—don't you think?" In the rearview mirror, the French sculptor discreetly shot her a cheerful look as she pressed down on the accelerator.

Abdollah's speech had reached its cosmo-mystico-megalomaniacal moment. He spread his arms wide:

"To all who remain in Iran. To all the people of my village. To all the women oppressed by the regime. And to everyone whose voice has been silenced, I say to you: I will be your voice. I'm here, in this world, to be your voice. Thank you for listening."

Carmina let out a long sigh and raised her imperious hand, demanding a chance to speak. Various inquisitive heads turned. Mona hunched over her notebook, wishing she could turn into a fox and dash off into the woods. Carmina leaned over to whisper something, but Mona couldn't understand a word of what she said. A round of applause ensued. The floor was open for a Q&A. Carmina stood up and raised her hand again. They brought her the microphone; she was impossible to ignore.

"I'm sorry, Abdollah, but you're not my voice. Don't you think it's presumptuous for you, a man, to give voice to the oppressed women in Iran, all because you had the good fortune to emigrate when you were young, and because you write and publish in the West? You, you of all men: *You're* the voice of the silenced? All those children, all those men and women who will never have a voice for as long as the regime endures—and you think you're going to give it back to them? You and your Dane-hypnotizing mustache? Abdollah Farid, tell me: Just who do you think you are?"

Before Abdollah had the chance to respond, an Israeli writer got ahold of the other mic and connected the discussion to the Holocaust. She spoke about the importance of giving voice to those who had lost their own: It's our mission as writers, she said, to bring to life what others are determined to stifle. Chrystos fluttered his eyelashes, a fronded corridor framing his iridescent pupils. His tears had only made him more beautiful, giving his eyes a dramatic shine.

"I think I need a drink," he whispered.

The Israeli writer, Hava Pinkus, passed the microphone to a man so white he looked almost albino. He introduced himself as Akto Perksson, one of the Nordic writers. The Meeting had its international contingent and its Scandinavian counterpart, a separate track that included half a dozen authors from Norway, Sweden, Denmark, and Finland, who were invited to make contributions to the international conversation on the legacy of Viking culture. Akto explained that he was a translator from Greek and Latin, as well as Finnish, but that recently he'd decided to write fiction in Swedish, which was why he felt it appropriate that he offer his comments in that language.

He then let loose a string of vowels that sounded like little wet explosions. The visiting authors put on their headsets for the simultaneous translation. The English interpreter used expressions like, *Well, you know*, in that sort of Great Plains accent that lends everything an affable and optimistic air. *Well, you know, I got run over by a truck. Well, you know, I've got two months to live.* Here was an artificial American sun rising over the phantasmagoric languages of Europe, that pregnant slut: *Well, you know, the past thirty years have been peaceful in Europe, and obviously we have to remain on the path to peace.*

Chrystos let his jaw drop like a cartoon character, and Mona knew right away that she'd found her gay sidekick for the festival. "I guess the only wars that matter are those that involve France, England, and the U.S.," Chrystos murmured. He handed back the pack of Kleenex.

There were Bosnia and Serbia, of course. And then there were Macedonia, Montenegro, the general *Yugoangst*. As though she were reading a friend's Facebook status out loud, Mona, whose mind had taken a backseat in her brain, surprised herself by saying, "War is everywhere." The words slipped out and took Chrystos a bit by surprise. The currents of an imperceptible pod of electric eels seemed to raise some hair in the little sea of heads before her. Was that what they were doing there, releasing imperceptible animals into the wild? But ideas ran the same risks within the mind as they did outside of it, after they were released. Or worse. In her head, for example, there was an entire school of piranhas just waiting to shred her ideas. Under the tent, everything the guests were writing in the air with their bodies could be captured on video: there was no such thing as the wild outdoors. Mona brought a hand to her neck, still wrapped in silk.

That was when she noticed that Philippe Laval, that sensation of French literature, was staring at her from the middle set of benches. They both hunched back down over their respective Moleskines. She'd read his first book, a comedy about an unusually intelligent boy who is traumatized by his experience at the École Normale Supérieure and leaves Paris for a life of noble reclusion in the countryside. Now, who would be the first victim of her charms? Mona looked around. The Alpine nonfiction writer was nowhere to be found.

The Q&A session ended with a big round of applause. The lady in stilettos was no longer at Mona's side. Abdollah had never answered her question. A true veteran of literary conferences, he'd allowed his listeners' own urge to speak to dominate the rest of the session. Chrystos adjusted the silk foulard around his neck and slid his finger along Mona's elbow.

"Who's publishing you in France?" he asked.

"Gallimard."

"Mmm, well done! I'm with Flammarion."

"Fantastic."

"Yeah, it's not Gallimard, but it's a good one."

When she saw he wanted her opinion on the subject, Mona smiled—Yeah, it's not bad—with calculated deference. It was actually kind of funny, she added, because her editor, Marianne Dubaut, had been Gabriel García Márquez's French translator for thirty years. Anyway, everything at Gallimard was done with the utmost attention and care. "Funny" and "not bad" were remnants of the English that she'd learned in American universities: a trail of trivial adjectives used to punctuate false modesty.

"Wow," Chrystos replied, "I'm so jealous. To be surrounded by that kind of energy. The energy of the Boom, the Boom generation—that's what they call it, right? Are those writers still so important to young people in South America? I think it's vital to surround oneself with grand personalities. Everything now is so . . . boring. Don't you think? It's like nobody cares about being a *personality* anymore. As if being a writer were no different from being a professor or a lawyer. It makes going to a writers' conference feel like attending a dental convention. That's what was so great about Abdollah: he didn't remind me of a dentist. Sorry if your parents are dentists! But I guess at the same time, personality can sometimes be something totally opaque, illegible. Have you met Ragnar yet, the Icelandic poet? You know his work? I sat next to him in the van and told him I admired his work—I said I admired it almost *too much*, because I'd read everything of his that ever came out in German (I used to have this boyfriend from Cologne, so I picked up some German—and there's worse things you can catch from a German boyfriend, right?). Anyway after a while Ragnar turned to me and said, 'I'm sorry, but it's not a good place'—the van, I guess—'to be a writer's writer.' He didn't talk to me the entire rest of the way. And he was awake the whole time—he didn't even try to hide it! He was just looking out the window. Isn't that funny? You think he has Asperger's? You think he'll win the Basske-Wortz? Part of me thinks that they brought us all here to be his courtiers, just to fill the place up. Because it's obvious that if they invited him *and he came* it's because they're giving it to him. Another part of me thinks, Great, I'd love to be part of his court. What do you think?"

What did Mona think? That her Alpine man, probable author of journalistic nonfiction, was very far away, talking to someone else, that he'd taken off his *Blade Runner* jacket, and that navy blue looked very good on him. But she said nothing. Chrystos and Mona left the tent with their empty mugs. Motionless over the lapis lazuli lake, a tenuous yellow star bade farewell as it faded into the day's slow heat. Chrystos had published a European bestseller on the family of Sigmund Freud, and clearly belonged to another league entirely—the league that actually sells books. Mona, on the other hand, was much more niche. The next talk was about to begin. "I'm going back to my cabin to write for a while," Mona said, blowing him a kiss.

"Seriously? You can write in the middle of one of these things? Well, I'm jealous. Have fun. Wait, I just remembered something. Please don't think I'm obsessed! I am, but just a little, and it's a normal kind of obsessed. It's about Ragnar. In the van, I watched him the whole way here—out of my peripheral vision, obviously, so I wouldn't piss him off. And I noticed something *really* weird. So, yeah, the Armenian poet yawned a few times during a conversation he was having with the Russian in front of me? And yawning's contagious. So I yawned, and Hava did, too. She was sitting next to me on the other side of the aisle. But Ragnar never yawned. Not once. You see where I'm going with this? He has no empathy reflex. The man is beyond all human ties. He exists in another sphere."

Mona started down the winding path that led back to the writers' quarters. They were all housed in rustic summer cabins. She remembered the room they'd assigned her was in a little duplex, two units connected by a small porch. But all of the cabins were dangerously similar, and she didn't recall which number was hers.

Mona inhaled deeply: the aroma of something like eucalyptus, the herbal freshness of the Swedish countryside. She fired up her vape and inhaled again, longer and slower this time. Through one cabin window, she saw the huge hairy back of someone facing a television. Another man was seated in front of him, semi-nude. Maybe Russians, Mona thought, looking away so that she wouldn't seem nosy. Some of the guests probably had to share rooms, an affliction so intolerable she could hardly imagine it. She tried to deduce the location of her cabin by facing the slope that led down to the lake and retracing her steps.

A small group of people was coming toward her. Five or six men, no more, in dark clothes, though the one leading the way was wearing a red sweater and holding some kind of staff. They might have been hikers, but the uniformity of the group caught Mona's attention. They looked like a soccer team or some kind of religious cult. Mona raised a hand to wave, but they veered into the woods without seeming to notice her.

Back in her cabin, Mona made sure the blinds were pulled. Then she settled down on the immaculate bed and opened her laptop. Two messages from Raoul, asking if she was okay. Missed calls from Antonio on practically all her messaging apps, and a photo of Franco's *cazzo*. She ignored them. Mona closed her eyes; her head was splitting. She got up to wash her face and spread a transparent green unguent over her skin. The snail mucus masque promised to reverse any dryness caused by airplane travel and hangovers. She kissed her vape a few times, then returned to the bed doubled over, coughing. With her laptop on her chest, she put on Mina's "Vorrei che fosse amore" and navigated to a porn site.

The videos started loading. Without really thinking about what she was doing, Mona opened another tab and started googling some of the other participants at the Meeting. She couldn't find anything about the Alpine nonfiction author. And beneath all the action, little green notifications kept lighting up—unanswered calls on Skype. Antonio again. Her novel-in-progress was also there, waiting for her, minimized at the bottom edge of the screen, far from the madding clicks.

In her open tab, a buff dude with an American haircut was massaging a redhead's pussy while a shorter guy ate her ass. She was a consummate professional, arching her back and neck for the camera, letting herself really get into it. Her hair hung down to her shoulders, swaying back and forth as she tossed her head and gazed off-screen, as though she weren't entirely present—as though her body parts weren't completely hers. It seemed like the redhead was performing her movements for someone beyond the frame, not for the camera or her partners. Mona liked to imagine the mental life of such moments, the connection between pleasure and "being somewhere else": skewered, and at the same time unreachable, inaccessible, sole guardian of a complex delight that wasn't trivially symmetrical to the body's adventures. A man, on the other hand, was always obliged to "be there," condemned to physical urgency and to being one with his cyclopean phallus. But pussies, no: they could drift, lunge, fill and empty themselves like voracious gluttons. And that was why—Mona sighed, settling into some dopamine-fueled theoretical masturbation—pussies were philosophical organs par excellence. A pussy puts the body right where philosophers evaded it: it was there innately open, happy to be perforated, grinded on, penetrated, flipped around—all while the intellect associated with that pussy performed its own secret, personal, and intimate revolution. She thought it was funny how even the #MeToo movement seemed to echo this private sentiment, at least lexically, spelling it out without spelling it out, since "#MeToo" could be pronounced *pound me too*, which in "Colonial" Spanish would translate to something like *dame masa a mí también*, destroy me, fuck me, too. But nobody seemed to notice, to be conscious of the linguistic underpinnings, and #MeToo had already passed into the annals of history as a synonym for emancipation and freedom.

At times the redhead almost seemed to be whispering something, speaking to someone only she could see, as in a classic case of hallucination. Her name was Naomi. Who was she talking to off-camera? Naomi. I MOAN, thought Mona, who always turned words over in her mind to see if they could mean something else. I think, therefore I moan. Would Naomi end up with bruises? How long do bruises last? The thought of a man dressed in black, watching Naomi from off-screen while the two other men gave it to her from behind, made Mona shudder.

Mona closed her eyes and lowered her panties. She sucked on her index and middle fingers before slowly introducing them to her interior world. She exhaled slowly, her body expectant before the nebulous arrival of pleasure—or the thought of it, which would come first.

Skype; incoming call. Was it possible that they'd read her manuscript? That fast? Upon the insistence of her editor, she had sent a draft of her second novel. Mona cleared her throat and double-checked the Band-Aid over the computer camera. All good.

"*Ça va*, Mona, *tout va bien*? Where are you, in New York?"

It was Myriam Legouleme, Mona's French translator. Ah, Sweden, the Basske-Wortz. She didn't know Mona had been nominated. *Bien!* chirped Myriam. Mona heard the dry rasp of a pencil against paper. *Oui oui*, Myriam and Marianne Dubaut herself had read it. With great interest. They had comments. Would she like to hear them now? Mona didn't have time to respond.

"Mona, the first thing I want to tell you is there's no need to be concerned. This happens to everyone."

"Why would I be concerned?"

"Really, it happens to everyone. It's every writer's second novel. You read it and think, Wow, where did that come from?"

Mona hesitated. Maybe she'd been in too much of a hurry to show them the manuscript. Maybe it hadn't yet become a novel. It was still a pupa, and the butterfly trapped inside the pupa was drying out, rotting without ever having been born, a fetus that wasn't alive, but wasn't exactly dead yet, either. The idea of something dying inside her made Mona feel a cold, throbbing pain, as though her body were a voodoo doll held in someone's frozen hand.

"Myriam, I'm really interested in your comments. I think it's really important that we have this conversation and that's why I wanted to show you some pages, a preliminary version, so that—"

But Myriam was no Yankee: putting on a show of goodwill and enthusiasm did nothing for her. Myriam was "no bullshit," with a French accent. Her lips must have been close to the mouthpiece because Mona could hear her breathing, the air flowing hot from the rancid cavern of her stomach.

"It's just that it's so . . . difficult! The characters are difficult. I kept asking myself, where is all the freshness and vitality of the first book? It's not *here*—that much I can tell you. The dialogue is practically incomprehensible. It made me ask myself, Am I really expected to make an effort to *understand*? Seriously? Why do I have to make such an effort? If I don't make the effort, am I just stupid, according to this book? Mind you, it's the novel that's posing these questions, not me."

"Well, I don't think the novel thinks you're stupid. I don't think any book would ever think that about you, Myriam."

"All jokes aside, Mona. Listen to me. Do you hear what I'm trying to tell you?"

"I don't know what to say, Myriam. I'm sorry you had to read something half-done. I didn't mean to bore you. I guess I was trying to be serious. I don't know."

"I don't think you have to give up on seriousness in your work—that's not it. Literature, whenever it's *vraie littérature*, is always serious. It's always serious. What you have to rethink is the opposition between life and non-life." *Life or non-life*, Myriam emphasized. "Because your characters are *dead*. They're *all dead*. And a novel is all about making them . . . *live*. So the question becomes, 'Why should I care about these people? They're so . . .' "

"Difficult?"

"Yes, difficult! But more than anything else, they're dead."

"Do you think they know they're dead?" Mona asked, somewhat surprised by her own question.

"What do you mean, like it's a zombie novel? Well, maybe they think they're alive, and maybe you think they are, too . . . but the writing just isn't there yet. That's the underlying issue: the writing is dead. But, like I said, don't get upset about it. It happens to the best. The second novel is always the hardest. And we have faith in you, both Marianne and I. You have to take your time, remember that nobody's trying to rush you. Your readers, they're expecting something from you. But not *this*. You can't give them this novel."

Myriam kept on in this vein, aspirating the final consonant whenever she said "this," as if it rhymed with *mépris*. Was she ever going to stop? Maybe Mona could just say she was about to go through a tunnel and lose the signal? Maybe she could just say, *Listen, Myriam, the internet connection is really bad here, can I call you later?* And then hide forever in the Swedish forest, lead a humble life, become like Bergman's Monika, triumphantly lost, vanishing without a trace.

She was imagining herself spreading honey across rustic rye bread, wearing a torn dress and tall rain boots, only to be interrupted by the melody of another incoming Skype call.

She'd dropped the connection and Myriam was calling back. Mona noticed her finger was still moist from her *sancta sanctorum*. She raised it to her nose so she could sniff it. Head lolling, eyes unfocused, like she was watching another scene, off-camera.

Myriam's voice occupied the whole room, but Mona couldn't follow her train of thought. Anyway, even if Myriam hadn't said so explicitly, Gallimard wasn't going to make an offer on her book. They wouldn't publish it ... not unless she took home the Basske-Wortz. You never can tell what a prize committee might do ... Mona knew that what she did (whatever it was) was considered *too intellectual* (or difficult) for her to achieve rapid commercial recognition. But the Basske-Wortz Prize, people said, operated outside the market—that is, outside the trivial criteria imposed by the market. Or at least Basske-Wortz himself was cited as saying, "The market doesn't exist because the market is imaginary, and the imagination is infinite, at least as long as the human race survives." The snail mucus had dried, leaving Mona's face cracked with gray fractals, like a girl from one of the bukkake porn channels. Flakes of peeling dried liquid hung from her face like little flaps.

Bisou bisou au revoir, and tell me when you're next in Paris, although we wouldn't want to interfere with your writing plans at all. Skype inquired whether Mona would like to rate the call (Excellent? Good? Normal?) and if she wanted to report any kind of problem with the connection. The Swedish summer light covered everything like a soft layer of dust, white material that made it look like it had just rained chalk. It was so cruel that darkness wouldn't start to fall until close to midnight. The day would remain in this pale limbo for interminable hours. It was a writers' purgatory, the white page as breathing air, where everyone was just waiting around to see who'd receive the key to paradise. How long do bruises last on the body?

5.

She applied eye makeup with professional dexterity. A violet shade across her eyelids, a pencil trace along the edge of the lower lid, and liquid eyeliner along the upper one, ending with a gentle curve toward the temples. Even though the diktats of makeup application held that false eyelashes should already be in place before a pencil ever comes near them, Mona preferred to draw the dark lines first and then apply the lashes. The eyeliner made it easier for them to stick. It wasn't the most efficient use of liquid eyeliner, since some of it inevitably went to waste, but it was how she liked it. She couldn't help it. She placed the strip of fake hairs across her eye and blinked a few times. Would they survive the sauna?

With YouTube on autoplay, her computer acted like a radio: an online news stream informed her about the disappearance of Sandrita, a twelve-year-old girl from the dangerous Lima neighborhood of Rímac. The screen displayed an older woman, humbly dressed—she must have been the mother—alongside another girl, probably an older sister, maybe about twenty. The daughter was the one responding to the questions. After a commercial break, the program host discussed the girl's disappearance with a psychologist. Mona was always taken aback by a Peruvian accent whenever she heard one: everyone reminded her of a kid in grade school, acting like the child they once were. In her little-girl accent, the psychologist on the news deliberated:

"We'll have to see if the girl stays missing. That is, if we're really talking about a missing person. Many victims of abuse go into hiding because they feel guilty about what happened to them, or because they're convinced that their abuser is still out there looking for them. Sometimes the abuser really is looking for them, but other times this impression is caused by the acute fear the victims feel, a fear that pushes them to hide, even when there is no further threat. These victims don't feel safe anywhere."

"But Sandrita is a little girl. You really think that she might be hiding? That Sandrita is avoiding her family on purpose, because she doesn't want to see them?" The newscaster seemed horrified by her own hypothesis.

"At the moment, all we have is a disappearance. We need to keep investigating."

Was she escaping? How could she know for sure? Mona coughed, her throat full of pure, artificial smoke from her vape. She looked in the mirror: no one would be able to tell by looking at her that she'd been crying, or how much alcohol she'd consumed. She slipped into a light silk dress and rain boots, put on her headphones ("Ela faz cinema," Chico

Buarque), and stuffed a bikini into her bag along with her Moleskine. Last but not least, she tied another handkerchief around her neck. The big bruise was still there, covered in BB cream. She closed her cabin door carefully, tangled in vape smoke and headphone cords. She took one step and then instinctively froze, leaning heavily on the banister.

A group of people dressed in black were standing there, looking down at something in the grass, some fifteen yards from her cabin. They were the same men she'd seen before, led by the blond with the red sweater and a staff. Were there wild tribes wandering Sweden, the way some cities have their own urban clans? Were these woodland bike-messenger boys? A sect of poetry fanatics? Ragnar's literary fan club? What were they doing there, staring at the grass? The blond in the red sweater was standing such that Mona saw him in profile, unable to see his whole face. Another blond in a sea of blonds. These Nordic blonds, her stoned mind reflected, are sort of like the Chinese, appearing all alike to outsiders. She leaned ruminatively against the banister, testing the philosophical soundness of her theory as she removed her phone from her pocket with the torpor of a drunk. The blond in red whispered something to the others, who now scampered off toward the forest like alert gazelles. *Hej! Adjö!* she called after them from afar. The photo captured them with their backs turned, already in motion. Mona moved toward the center of their empty circle. There, lying in the grass, was a fox with her throat slit. Her little red eyes gazed back at Mona, calm and cold.

She took off at top speed, away from the forest and toward the white tent and Patrick Hus, the Meeting's social hub. Whenever she cried, the tears left a film over her corneas, casting luminous sparkles across the visible world. Her heart beat strong. She was shaking and needed to calm down. Had the fox even seen her predator? Had he stalked her through the forest? Had she stared down her killer? Had she begged for mercy? Whoever killed the fox had left her body in the broad light of the interminable day. Remorseless, shameless. Forcing her way forward, Mona dragged herself toward a knot of writers conversing on the gravel. Her interactions had been minimal to this point. She'd only spoken with Snorri, Chrystos, and the Korean woman from the van—which made her a bit nervous. What would happen if she tried to speak to them but made no sense, if what came out of her mouth was a gush of nonsense that soon trailed off into silence?

Seeing her approach, the little circle of writers opened into a welcoming *C*. There was Chrystos, the Macedonian author, and Carmina, the *donna italiana* who'd taken Abdollah to task, and who now introduced herself to Mona as a bestselling writer of Albanian extraction who now lived in Rome. Are you from Argentina? the Israeli writer asked. Ah, Peru! Machu Picchu! Had she been to Machu Picchu? Mona tilted her head up and back, then down and forward, before rolling it from side to side, which left it unclear whether she was responding yes or no—but she managed to make the bones in her neck crack. It's marvelous, Hava told her, having taken Mona's gesture to mean she'd never been. You have to go!

"We were just saying that it seems like they're going to take us to the lake tonight!"

Hava was organizing a human rights conference. She wrote poems about Israel, the kabbalah, and the Holocaust. She taught university courses on feminism, literature, and human rights, and was coordinating a literary symposium while she pursued her doctorate. She lived in Jerusalem and had edited two anthologies of women writers who compiled testimonies of family members who'd survived the Holocaust. She explained that the cultural memory of what happened had just begun to cohere, having skipped a generation. Forget Primo Levi and those guys! It was only now, she explained, that people felt like they could really talk about it. This was Hava's discovery, although she didn't make it out to be her own, presenting it instead as a self-evident fact. It was obvious, she droned on, that the question of the Holocaust had become more urgent than ever: bad things sometimes stay trapped inside the mind, which cannot expel them until they're finally expressed.

"Sometimes I go for walks in Tel Aviv near where the army boys are stationed, or to the beach where they go to drink beer. My god! I don't know what I would've done as a girl if I knew anything about sex at that age. Or if the internet existed back then! *Chas v'shalom!* The sex that you can find through the internet, my god, don't get me started. Let's not get into it!"

Warming to her theme, and whipping up her audience like an expert talk-show host, Hava turned to Carmina, the Italo-Albanian writer.

"What about you? How old were you when you first discovered sex?"

"Hava! You're terrible. C'mon, why don't you ask me?" Chrystos proposed, adjusting the blue-green foulard around his neck.

"Wow, you guys, are you really so scandalized? It's just a question!" Hava shrugged, turning her palms to the sky, clearly delighted. "But yes, Chrystos, darling, I want you to tell me everything, of course. I want to hear all your fantasies about Jesus. We could have a whole session about our sexual experiences, something outside the official conference program and organized by us, as participants. The director told me they're open to any sort of activity we want to propose, and there's already an open mic scheduled. We could even do it tonight—at the lake!" Hava shaped the first part of her sentence as a question, but ended with a sharp spike of enthusiasm.

"Finally, a proposal that makes sense has emerged from this festival of ideas." The Alpine turned to Mona. "Hi, I'm Sven." From two feet away, he was exponentially more handsome.

Sven said hi to everybody in the C while Mona squeezed his outstretched hand and returned a friendly, slightly timid, smile. At last, the nonfictionalist. It had been a long time, she thought, since she'd been around a man who smelled so good. She caught notes of leather, coffee, and citrus in his cologne, and something like eucalyptus on his breath. He seemed freshly shaved. His lambskin *Blade Runner* jacket looked soft, like it might bleat softly if she stroked it, although it was evident that no actual sheep had suffered in the process of clothing him. After releasing her hand, Sven winked and calmly walked away to join another group of writers. Had he done that on purpose, said hello and then wandered off like that? She hoped so. It was so amusing that Mona found her lips involuntarily blossoming into a smile.

"Why don't we just do a whole TED Talk about it?" Carmina quipped.

Hava's countenance darkened. She narrowed her eyes into a practiced shrewish glare and began to issue strenuous objections.

"No, please, there's nothing I hate more than TED Talks. They've ruined the world! Look, I've been going to scientific conferences for decades. They can be boring sometimes, depending on the audience and the speaker, of course. But at least there's *something* there. Ever since people got wrapped up in that cultural emphysema called a TED Talk, everyone just goes around saying the same thing. Exactly the same thing! How can everyone have the same life? Everybody starts by telling some stupid story about when they were a kid. Then some defining event happens to them, and they dedicate the rest of their lives to responding to the needs and inadequacies of the child they once were, and the audience gets all emotional and filled with a sense of wonder and applauds like crazy when it's finally over. As if the narrative for someone's personal calling *always* has to sound so stupid!"

Everyone laughed. Mona wanted to tell them about the fox she'd found dead in the field, but she didn't know how. About ten yards away, Sven was rolling a cigarette as he talked with Abdollah and a tall boy who looked a bit like Frankenstein's monster—he was a poet from Latvia, she recalled from the program—and a pale and beautiful young woman who, judging by her minimalist modern look, seemed like she came from the Netherlands, or maybe lived in Berlin. Mona saw herself leaving Hava's talk show, walking off set with the lights still bright, drawn to Sven's lambskin jacket, whispering in his ear: *I just saw a dead fox.* With one burst of extroversion she could cut the knot that cinched her throat. But she was too high to move. Her attention returned to the talk show: Chrystos, Carmina, and Hava. She wouldn't be able to communicate how she felt by telling them what she saw. And besides that, she felt guilty for having left the fox's body where it was. Should she propose that they all go see it together? And what if it wasn't there anymore? What if they'd already taken it away? They'd think she was crazy. Hava's fervent tone awakened her:

"Science sometimes has a *narrative* and can even be *personal*, I get it. But there's no blood in it anymore, no impulsivity, no quest. And what does it mean for us to obey the seven-year-old child inside us? That our bosses are basically all seven-year-olds talking at us from behind their twenty-two-year-old faces? There's nothing left but capital-ism! There are no other narratives!"

"Funny you should mention that, Hava. I was just saying something similar to Mona this morning: that there are no real personalities anymore. The era of great writers, the real *artists*—"

"It's because there's no blood in it anymore!" Hava was exasperated. She turned to Mona and abruptly changed the subject: "*Tarrile-Byrne*—what kind of name is that? Are you Jewish?"

Mona was the talk-show guest who gave a timid smile whenever the attention was focused on her, dissembling her desire to escape.

She mentally reviewed the list of strange women who populated her bloodline, their fluids pouring down from the Andes in an illiterate mudslide. She pictured those places on earth where the ground comes undone and goes verti-cal, where the range breaks into pieces that come loose and fall from high above, rolling vertiginously for miles until they smash into the sea. That was her home, and it wasn't mate-rial for small talk. Her great-grandmother married an Irish Catholic with sky-blue eyes, a drunk who regularly beat her; her grandmother had tried to escape her own marriage, but ended up with a man who treated her like a slave, shackled to ten children. And still Mona remembered her grandfather as a kindly little man. But Mona didn't want to sound too intense, not at this time of day, and certainly not without the comforting companionship of friendly benzos and elegant alcohols. Although she'd been raised on Catholic pomp and circumstance, she explained, she'd always *wished* she were Jewish, for reasons that were too long and complicated for her to explain. Mona grew up in a rural, almost medieval world, whereas the Latin American Jewish universe was typically urban and cosmopolitan—and she'd always desired the city and civilization. She'd studied biblical Hebrew for two years. Her study group had translated passages from Bereshit and Ruth.

"Anyway, my family is Irish and Portuguese on my father's side, and native Peruvian on my mother's side. No matter how far you go back, it's just more illiterate Catholics. So I'm sorry to disappoint you, Hava: there's not a trace of anything Jewish in me."

Hava beamed her a wide smile.

"Oh dear. You're young and, pardon me for saying so, somewhat naive. Let me tell you something: *of course* you're part Jewish. This interest of yours, in being Jewish? Where do you think that came from? You think it came from the internet, like some kind of virus? It's innate. It's something you know about yourself, even if it's hidden, just waiting for the right moment to come to the surface. Like memories of the Holocaust, just waiting to emerge. Our memories look down at us from their precipice, letting us live our normal lives—or almost normal. But there's a volcano underneath, just waiting to erupt. I feel them watching us—I feel my memories watching me. And didn't you know that the majority of the Spanish and Portuguese people who ended up in America were incognito Jews, forced to convert and live as Marranos? Anyway . . . have any of you read that Icelandic author that everyone's talking about?"

The Meeting was still on break, but the sessions would soon start up again. Groups of writers slalomed along the path that connected the cabins to the big tent. She didn't see Sven, the Alpine journalist who shielded his eyes with what looked like a newspaper whenever he laughed. She mentally corrected herself: she shouldn't call him a journalist, just in case. The respected term was "literary nonfiction." Practitioners of the genre took it very seriously, especially the ones who wrote "personal essays" that reported on their "personal truth" in the post-truth era. They were all quite sensitive. As she drifted away from Hava's group, Mona blew them a kiss, the drone of all goodbyes.

"Sorry, guys, just remembered I left my cigs in the cabin."

"All right, then," Hava called out, "we'll see you at the next session—or at the lake!"

The kinetic drive of her escape had decided things. The ruminative phase of the trip was over: next came the real fooling around. By this she didn't refer to any specific regimen; she certainly didn't intend to make a fool of herself, as a literal translation might indicate: *ser tonta en los alrededores*—although that was always a possibility. No, in situations like this one, the expression could mean any number of things, anything from no-strings-attached seductions to merely allowing herself to be invaded by a jovial spirit of playfulness—she'd *irse en yolo*, as they said in Lima, or what in Argentina they called *hacer cualquiera*. In international waters, without a compass: at times like these, with no other task than simply *to be*, even if being was nothing more than being a *cocotte*, a being fundamentally without any ties, and therefore without limitations, but nevertheless (and more than ever) a woman, Mona embraced her liberty the way the blind embrace the darkness. It was merely her element, impossible to avoid. The Meeting (and its double, the fantastic proximity of the Basske-Wortz Prize and its portentous ability to transform her life) was an opportunity to commune with Life with a capital *L*, along with all of the luxurious mysteries that the Authentic Life must contain.

Mona strolled along a corridor of conifers that separated the cabins from the social side of the resort. She'd skipped several meals, but her cigarettes, so out of fashion, helped her forget about eating—and that was always in style. She wasn't sure she'd taken the right path, but in her mind she could already taste the Swedish sauna, which she imagined to be similar to the *banya* she'd tried in Moscow. The Russian bath was just a dumpy gray building on the outside, but inside it opened into a magnificent oval room, with moldings from the time of the czars. She'd gone with her friend Ilona, and when they arrived they were each handed large branches of eucalyptus. The two of them paraded down the *banya*'s marble hallways like a pair of debutantes. The building was a luxury bathhouse that had been converted into a Soviet gymnasium and then back into a luxury bath. Sticking together, Mona and Ilona installed themselves in a corner and stripped down to their bikinis. When they saw that the locals just went around nude, their hair swept up into turbans filled with herbal tinctures to make it fragrant and smooth, Mona and Ilona shrugged at each other and took off their bikinis. The Russian women were slathered in homemade ointments made with honey, which gave their arms and legs a surreal, dazzling sheen. But what Mona most remembered was the way they stared at her wherever she went, almost offended by her presence.

At first glance it seemed obvious that, to the Russians, this thing they had before them—which is to say, Mona (because she'd gotten used to thinking of herself as an object)—was a species native to Mato Grosso: an exotic being, primitive and savage. Mona was an Amazonian island, the human stain licked by every gaze. Had they no manners? Why were they staring like that? Mona pretended to be scandalized. Adopting the role of her protector, Ilona offered comfort by scraping her eucalyptus branch across Mona's back. She was delighted to play the part of the white slave to Mona, the dark nymph. Why can't they take their eyes off me? On the improvised throne provided by the stairs descending into the pool, recovering from the extremely high temperatures, her skin aflame and each of her tiny veins an incandescent red, Mona stared back at the Russians before finally averting her gaze. As she perched on a marble stair, Mona's very own unshaved Mato Grosso was shining like a spongy tarantula, an omniscient and all-seeing eye. Later on, a certainty coiled around her vanity: they were staring because they'd never seen anything like her.

But she had the Swedish sauna to herself. A small dressing room fitted with mirrors and badly lit with dim fluorescent bulbs adjoined the boiling-hot wooden box. Mona unwrapped the handkerchief from around her neck, took off her dress, removed her contacts, and wrapped herself in a somewhat threadbare towel she found on a bench. She stepped into the sauna and settled onto the highest level. Sweaty and salty, supine over her curves, she hoped the nucleus of her pain (which remained hidden deep in her interior, as Hava had said) would overflow, dripping down to create sharp stalagmites rising out of her inner morass. Pain was like excess fat, or a retained liquid that would eventually find a way to flow free and exit her body. She closed her eyes and imagined herself, skin shining like a velvety orchid in the sauna's thin pine shell. A man would come in and start eating her out, with a hunger emerging from deep inside. She would await him, motionless, like certain Andean flowers when they sense the desperate thirst of an approaching insect. A man dressed in black. A man dressed in black with something she couldn't quite make out in his hand. A staff. And she would just tilt her head back against the wood and let herself be ravished. At first she wouldn't be able to separate pleasure from terror. Her skin would burn with each little thrust, until she finally felt the freshness of the grass, unconscious beneath the trees. Like the little fox, like Sandrita (even though nobody knew where Sandrita was). A groundskeeper would find her nearly lifeless, take her home, and clean her wounds. Mona started to tense up and then release without changing position. Most of her masturbation sessions started out this way. She was a total nympho for terror.

A voice boomed inside the sauna: "Hello!"

A man was there, smiling at her. He shook out a towel that was completely soaked in sweat and wrapped it around his head. Taken aback, Mona covered herself immediately with her towel. He'd been there the entire time, seated on the first level. His pubic hair was shining like an illuminated forest, traversed by a large white worm.

Without her contacts, Mona's sauna companion was just an out-of-focus mass. Her fantasies tended to populate themselves avidly, but this was a moment she could have done without an audience. Mona took a breath and said hi.

"Pleased to meet you. My name's Akto. Sorry if I don't say much, it's just that at conferences like these I have a hard time writing, and if I get to talking I'll write even less. It's that way all the time: my writing is inversely proportional to my speech."

He pulled the towel back down over his face. Akto was the Swede who'd given a talk earlier that day in the tent. When she was on the point of fainting, Mona took a deep breath and left the sauna. She sat down in the dressing room to recover from the extreme heat. She enjoyed the feeling of barely being in control of her own body, reduced to raw survival: feeling the tumult of her afflicted organs, her expanded heart thudding away. She stepped into the cold shower. An intense, minutes-long shiver left her trembling and spent. Then the lights went out completely, and for a second Mona thought she'd finally fainted.

A woman's voice: "Mona, right?"

The voice was coming from a corner of the dressing room: a bulky shape in the shadows. "Yes, it's you. Remember me? We met in Lyon."

Mona sensed someone coming toward her while her neck rolled like pudding, her tongue lapping against the roof of her brain.

"I was your interpreter. The Lyon literary festival."

Mona blinked. The TGV, never-ending fog on both sides of the tracks. The train penetrating the gray suburbs of an industrial city, the oblique sun shying away from the depressing buildings. *La France, la France c'est un jardin*: her editor's husband had used this nasal phrase to describe what she'd see on the journey. Nuclear fallout, not a soul in the streets.

The woman twisted a switch and the tungsten tubes overhead reactivated, flickering and hissing. Mona recoiled, as if the light might burn her. With a sizzle, one of the tubes suddenly burned out, leaving a flickering shadow between the yellow light streaming in through a vent and the lone tube still glowing, hidden at the back of the room. Backlit in this fashion, she was all the more impressive. Pale, and with long dark hair, the speaker standing before Mona was a tremendously fat woman, draped in a red robe.

"Remember? I'm a writer now. I write children's books."

"Oh, how nice." Mona smiled back at her, but then remembered her own nakedness, her body telling a story she didn't know how to put into words. She tried to cover herself with her discarded towel. "Are the books illustrated? Do you draw, too?"

Lena's face twisted, hardening into a scowl. She replied with excruciating slowness, as though it took every ounce of her patience to remain civil: "Well, yes, I work with an artist. But I guess you don't consider children's books to be real literature, do you?"

"I never said that. In fact, I love Roald Dahl . . ."

Mona choked on the surname, as though the *h* had stuck in her throat. Roald Dahl was a faux pas: there were films based on his stories. He was too mainstream to be mentioned among seminude peers at a literary conference. She took a minute to mentally google the covers of other children's books, but her search came up without results.

". . . Well, congratulations on being translated! Into Swedish, I mean."

"Yeah, I won the Baltic Prize for best children's book. A lot of money. I invited you to the class I teach at the university but you had a cold and couldn't come. I'm Lena Bactreau. The name rings a bell, right?"

"Congratulations, Lena. What a pleasure to see you again."

Mona started to let down her guard. Now that the woman had established her pedigree, it was simply a matter of letting her talk about herself, and everything would be fine. Mona sat up to dry her hair. Lena's intense eyes flashed with their own light in the dressing-room gloom, like emergency flares.

"I remember that day in Lyon," Lena continued. "You were wearing a sweatshirt. A Kenzo sweatshirt," she added, in an accusatory tone.

Mona detected a Madrid accent, a detail that helped her reconstruct Lena's personal history. Originally from Bordeaux, Lena had summered in Spain ever since she was fifteen. She'd embraced the Spanish language the way someone might insinuate themselves into an ideal family. Her youth had coincided with Spain's adoption of the euro and the transformation of Barcelona in preparation for the Olympics. It was the moment Spain launched its rebranding, in all its grandeur—and without the cycle of lamentations, protests, and *indignados* that were still to come after the eruption of the 15-M protests. By the time the mortgage crisis rolled around, Lena had already adopted a Castilian accent and persona—only a whiff of her provincial French remained—as well as that vigor in her gaze, so Iberian, a force that could translate well into staccato heels on wooden boards, hot peppers and nervous breakdowns à la Almodóvar—or a Basque separatist bombing, whatever the occasion demands. Now Lena gave Spanish classes at a university, having dedicated her life to personifying the Spanish nation.

"You really have a prodigious memory, Lena. I don't

remember what I was wearing, but I'm sure you're right. I love that sweater."

"We went to the bathroom together, before the panel, and I told you my life story."

"And now we're in the sauna together!" Mona tried to stand up again, her head still heavy.

With a mix of disdain and disinterest, Lena examined the bashful spectacle of Mona, still carefully wrapped in her towel, with another hanging from her neck. Mona approached the vanity to put in her contacts and use the hair dryer. With any luck, that would kill the conversation. But Lena wasn't deterred.

"That day we had a conversation. A very interesting one." Lena allowed a dramatic pause to elapse. "We decided that writing was monstrous."

"I said that?"

"We both did."

With calm exasperation, Lena lifted an arm, running her five fingers through her hair like a wide comb. "We said we didn't know if what we were doing was living our lives or just feeding the monster. That the earth's crust is like the surface of a frozen lake, but beneath it there's this giant eye, watching. And life is a journey across the ice, knowing that it's there, watching you, stalking you. Everything you do is touched by the knowledge that the monster is watching and waiting. What's left of you if you don't write about it? Do you live for yourself or for the monster who writes? Your brain wages secret wars against the lifeless movie of your life. It *secretes* these wars against life. You remember all this?"

Mona nodded in silence. She'd even written something along those lines, but off the page it sounded murky and odd—like the rest of her feelings lately.

Lena paused to unfasten her red robe. With her lenses back in, Mona could tell that Lena was wearing a dark thong whose straps disappeared into the rolls of flesh that descended in waves from her vigorous tits, their pointy nipples resting against her belly. Lena looked like something was lurking inside her, too, as though her body was inhabited by something unhinged and razor-sharp—or maybe by several of those somethings. Mona caught her breath, the hair dryer still purring on low.

"Because, as women, we're in touch with the monstrous. All the time. You, with your over-the-top makeup, your too-red lips—and you're wearing fake eyelashes, right? See, you went to the sauna with lip liner on, like you're some kind of clown or a model, which you're not, of course—you're certainly no model! And me, I'm obese . . . We can agree that I'm obese, right? It's not normal to get this fat. Or do you think this sort of thing *just happens*?"

She waited for Mona to corroborate her observations.

"Okay, but who are we to say what's norm—"

A shiver of scorn crossed Lena's face, an allergic reaction to bullshit.

"Don't play the fool with me. I don't have time to talk about what's *normal*. The human body wasn't engineered to

82

be like *this*, and you know it. You can't deny it. It's simple: We are, in our era, conscious that humanity is an animal in the process of extinction. So the search for perfection is in no way mundane or superficial. What we consider anorexia is a social exercise for how the human race can survive when there's no food left—for how to have the best chances of survival as a species. The people who die of it are modern martyrs."

Lena's words blew through Mona like a chill breeze. She was left with an image: *Homo sapiens* suspended by a thread between earth and the void—until the earth's round form, wearing Lena's fat face, began to rotate away, her gaze lost in outer space. Mona admired Lena's lack of self-regard, the blunt rationalism she exercised in speaking about herself, cold and powerful as an iceberg. How different the world would be if Lena were allowed to reorganize it. Mona imagined her giving the species a real shake-up: Medusa in a bikini, thrusting *Homo sapiens* into a dungeon it could only escape by surrendering to her desires, like the perverse head Nazi from Lina Wertmüller's *Seven Beauties*, a film that had always fascinated her. On the other hand, this fat power trip, Lena's exultant obesity—it was the only sensible minority position within reach of a white Frenchwoman. And Lena *had* managed to make her feel a bit bad about herself, which Mona always figured was every fat woman's secret objective. But the truth was that Mona had no problem taking this particular bullet. She accepted humiliations with instinctive courtesy; any kind of guilt made her feel good. She considered it a noble exchange, with herself in the role of martyred Saint Sebastian.

"What I mean is this: these distortions are a way of being in the world and of no longer tolerating it. That's why we transform ourselves like drag queens. Look at you. Yes, you. You're a complete caricature of a woman. Have you looked at yourself? You're completely ridiculous. Covering yourself with that towel, like anyone cares what you're hiding underneath it. Tell me what kind of woman gets in the sauna wearing fake eyelashes. Or do you think that nobody can tell? With your makeup, your designer clothes, your hyper-feminine affect . . . you think that you're letting everyone see that you're a victim of machismo, of a chauvinist culture that—even with its little touches of sophistication, like the literary world!—punishes all things feminine. But that doesn't annul the total *absurdity* of your appearance. Don't kid yourself—you're certainly not fooling me! Where I'm going with all this is: We can't write except in drag. We convert ourselves into something absurd because the absurd is already living inside us."

Mona continued getting dressed, undaunted. "Are you saying that we're condemned to play the part of monsters because we're writers?" The thing about the eyelashes had hurt her feelings a little—her eyes were her Achilles' heel—but she repressed all signs of emotion. If the majority of people went their whole lives without ever understanding the sources of their own pleasure, Lena, as a citizen of the land of the overweight, had found a shortcut to the wellsprings of her own. And her pleasures had become a commitment, a way of life. Someone as fat as Lena could just roll through society like a Panzer, or else lie in wait for unsuspecting writers at isolated cabins in the woods, like the heroine-reader of *Misery*.

Lena continued with excitement: "When I say we play the part, what I mean is that *we live it*. We embrace it without realizing it. And then we become it. It's not enough to play the part in our heads. We're forced to go beyond our minds—we're obliged to *incarnate* these personae. And there's nothing as womanly as incarnation. To be a woman and write is to be trans. That's why writing is trans, being fat is trans, and this whole entire performance of being a woman is the most trans thing in the world. Ever since Tiresias, who of course was the first trans person ever."

Mona glanced up at Lena's reflection in the mirror. Her fists were clenched, her neck curved like a wild boar's. Lena stared back without blinking.

"And you know what else? There's no place for women in literature, either. There's nowhere for them—nowhere, and we know it. And that's why we make ourselves into freaks: we react and adapt to the state of things instinctively. We're not so different from Julian of Norwich, who wanted to be a saint so badly that she became a little indie nun, God's only lover. And why'd she do it? So that they'd leave her alone to write in her cloister, glory to God in heaven. Or Margery Kempe, who made herself an outsider in her own family—a ridiculous woman in red socks, as Chaucer described her—just so she could escape this world and flee into her own, where at last she'd be able to write. Her caves and grottoes are your makeup and my obesity: they're our unnatural way of being in the world. Are you married?"

"No."

"You have a boyfriend? Sorry if I'm being intrusive." For the first time, Lena laughed.

No, you're not being too intrusive, Mona thought, you're just an intense fat lady who's determined to give me a headache. She wrapped her towel around her shoulders as if it were a cashmere shawl and smiled.

"No, no, it's fine."

There was a hiss, like a hermetic container being unsealed. It was Akto opening the heavy wooden door to the sauna. How could she have forgotten that he was still in there? Had he heard them? Naked and red as a tomato from the heat, he greeted them each with a slight inclination of his head.

"Sorry if I don't shake hands. Mine's all sweaty," Akto explained conscientiously. He approached Lena, caressing his head with his wadded-up hand towel, still dripping with perspiration. "I started out translating from Latin and Greek, and sometimes from Swedish and Finnish, but recently I decided to start writing fiction. We haven't met yet. You're here for the Meeting, too, right? What's your name?"

The women were silent. Akto was making eye contact with Lena, who gravely sustained it while Akto dried his head and went on, oblivious and smiling, to recommend

86

nearby hikes and lakes. There was humility to his nudity, and nothing offensive or sexual about it. It was almost as though his manhood had renounced *tout court* any right to address them, either through amorous overtures or a show of brute strength. Maybe Akto was simply the purified product of those gigantic Nordic goddesses, who for millennia crouched over the region's fjords, straddling the living geography and letting the juices run from their divine pussies like acids coursing across the unformed earth, shaping everything in their wake (the fjords, the grasslands, humankind) with their image and likeness, according to their tastes and pleasures. The privilege with which Akto paraded his penis around, combined with that one-note voice: they were parallel traits that knew no shame or silence. It was clear that this in itself could offend Lena, but so long as Akto didn't give off any threatening vibes or brandish his cock or his arrogance in their faces, could he still be said to be a man, one of the patriarchy's agents? And if he wasn't, to what new species would he belong? Was Akto trans, too? Mona wanted to ask, but Lena might explode at any moment. Her teratological feminism hadn't prepared her for an Akto. She seemed to lack any theories to apply when faced with a man who appeared to be as inoffensive as he was nude. Mona's eyes darted around the dressing room for her clothes and her bag, somewhat afraid of what Lena might do next. Akto and Lena didn't even hear the door close: Mona slid out of view on tiptoe, her dress still balled up in her hand.

6.

She stole into the pine forest surrounding the cabins. She put on her panties: they were a bit loose, and she could feel the smoothness of her labia as she walked, her legs creating a swish of air as she strode onward. She smelled like celery and sweat, something fresh and tart, herbal—like she'd spent hours rolling around on the ground, perfuming herself with the pheromones of the earth.

She took a generous toke from her vape. The green liquid bubbled with excitement over its transformation into another substance. She could feel all the darkness in the world concentrated in the depths of her throat. The trees towered overhead, closing in like a cocoon, protecting her from the deathly white of a world in which all things obeyed the will of the sun. The cold air tightened her cheeks and reminded her of her nudity. She scampered further into the forest.

She saw herself as a wild animal, a joyous arrow darting between patches of darkness and green. She ran until she hurt herself, the branches lashing her face, as though the trees were reaching down to scrape her with their lugubrious hands. The scent of evergreens was so powerful that she felt nauseated. Mona stopped to catch her breath and sensed there was someone watching her. The trees kept their own counsel. Had someone followed her? Something was stirring in the bushes. She was moving slowly now, but her heart beat faster. Her hand came to rest on an ancient trunk. She dug her fingernails into the bark until she felt a rush of pain. Her labia had dilated from all the running. She slipped a finger inside, very slowly, and noticed that she was completely wet. A special elixir, released by sudden terror in an unfamiliar location, her thudding heart. She thought she could hear the rushing of a nearby stream.

Still feeling the pain under her fingernails, Mona dug further into the bark with her free hand, until one of her fingertips produced a drop of blood. She stopped to remove the splinter. The blood would give away her location—the scent of prey. Like the fox. The fox would have known that she was marked as prey. Had she sensed her predator's excitement when her hunter smelled its quarry? Or did fear cloud all else, disintegrating all sensations until they became unrecognizable? Is there such a thing as lucid terror? She, too, had secreted something irresistible, excited by fear. It was a way of losing herself. Smelling a bit of blood and wanting more.

She strolled among the bushes until something caught her attention: a curved row of stones, bifurcating to make a lined path. The rock path brought her to a mass of boulders covered by lichen. Possibly an animal's lair. Mona felt herself attracted to the opening in the rocks, as if she'd once emerged from that cave and was compelled to return. Was there any light, any kind of reflection that would allow her to see inside? She stuck her head inside the cave and felt the temperature drop. A chill passed through her. She fished her phone out of her bag and lit the flashlight. Something was moving within view of the cavern's opening. Could it be him? Had he lured her here? Vertigo throbbed in her veins like the sweat creeping over her skin. Her foot sank into something sticky and wet. She held fast to the rocks to keep from sliding. She directed the beam of her flashlight downward, to see what it was beneath her twisted foot: the little head of a decapitated animal, its dark fur caked with blood.

She took off running from the cave. There was clearly something moving in the foliage now. She heard breathing.

A flash of light between the leaves—the sun glancing off the dial of a watch. Mona squinted through the bushes at what looked like Chrystos, naked but for his boots. He was on his knees, blowing a lumberjack.

She spirited herself away as quickly as she could. Safely ensconced in a private grove, she switched off the flashlight on her phone and reconnected to the network. She'd had her phone back in airplane mode to avoid interruptions and to ensure she remained the sole guardian of her solitude. Tons of mentions on Twitter and Facebook, mostly from followers she didn't even know. She just wanted to see if there were any new insults. Appeals to retweet updates on Sandrita, the girl who'd been abducted in Lima. Sandrita was wearing a pair of black shorts and a white sweatshirt the last time anybody saw her in Rímac. Mona had only been there on a brief, co-ordinated visit with a specific destination: the house where her mother was born. She didn't want to see the photo of Sandrita—she wanted to avoid the memory that had been haunting her, yet as she pushed it out of her mind she felt so many eyes upon her, the eyes of other little girls. She didn't want to remember, and reflexively hit *retweet*.

There were a few missed calls, too. One from her friend Mathilde, who was asking after a few short poems to be read as a voice-over in an Hermès commercial. The others were from Franco and Antonio. Fucking Antonio. She let out a huff and tried to concentrate on Mathilde, who'd promised her an Hermès scarf as payment for the poems. It was a gig Mona had forgotten about entirely.

She stormed into Patrick Hus and made straight for the buffet, piling moussaka and house salad onto her plate. A hot tea, a miniature bottle of water. This would give her enough energy to write. It was well past lunchtime and the majority of the writers were still busy attending talks or back in their cabins—or fellating new friends in the woods. At a nearby table, a woman was seated before a book and a cup of tea. It was the Japanese writer Shingzwe. She was impeccably dressed, all in white, with a buttoned white piqué cardigan, a small cameo poised between the lapels. Her delicate hands rested on the table.

Without thinking too much about it, Mona approached with her sloppy dish of food. It had been years since she'd first heard of Shingzwe, and she'd followed her career with curiosity, through the sporadic publication of her poems in literary magazines. Her single name, itself a strange incongruity, was a provocation that no one would have expected from such an elegant woman. She wanted Shingzwe to know that she adored a poem of hers that she'd read online the night before, about a bowl and some grains of rice.

Shingzwe thanked Mona with an inclination of her head and invited her to sit down. She said it was the first time she'd ever met a writer from Peru in person, although she'd gotten to know Vargas Llosa many years prior. I mean the first woman writer, she said with a smile.

Mona set her plate down on the table, feeling like she possessed all the subtlety of an elephant in comparison to the delicate air of refinement that surrounded Shingzwe. Her coiffed hair was arranged in a perfect pom-pom, and a silk handkerchief in lilac and pale pink made a perfect V over her shoulders. Shingzwe held her head erect, her mouth immobilized in a half smile. The Japanese writer made a gesture meant to encourage Mona to eat. Mona lowered her lips down to the moussaka rather than lift it to her mouth. She didn't want to look up, because she knew Shingzwe was silently watching her, and she couldn't help feeling clumsy in her presence. Shingzwe would be the perfect choice for the Basske-Wortz: at the prize ceremony, she'd limit her remarks to reading a long poem about the sky, a word-painting in which the clouds would move like giant ships, magnificent as they crossed the blue expanse. And the minds that took in the poem would likewise feel that expanse, and delight in their union with that immensity, listening to the story of two cumulonimbus clouds buffeted by savage winds sweeping shadows across the sea. After a flawless performance, Shingzwe would take the money and go home without a fuss. She was the ideal winner, the contrapuntal yin to Ragnar's dark yang—Ragnar, everybody's hands-on favorite. It was lucky, Mona thought, that Shingzwe was a poet and not a novelist. Because, if not, and given the circumstances, she could destroy Mona by writing about her in one of her novels. Since that wasn't the case, Mona could let her hair down: nothing she said would leave their table. And if some remark did make it into one of her poems, it would be in the shape of a feeling impossible to trace back to the specter of Mona now seated before her, arm trembling as she tried to handle her silverware, tears springing uncontrollably from her eyes. There was nothing she could do to stop them.

Mona leaned back in her chair, put down her fork, and slowly dabbed her eyes and wiped the edges of her mouth with her napkin, engaged in a colossal struggle against her lack of control.

"Shingzwe, as no doubt you've noticed, I'm crying. I can't tell you why, because I don't know. I don't know why I'm here. I only know that I am here, with you, and that I can't write. But it's not just that. There's something in me . . ."—here Mona brought a hand to her chest—"I don't know what it is, but it hurts, it burns like some kind of shame, and there's nothing I can do about it."

Shingzwe nodded. "You have a pure heart. I can see it. A pure heart is rare in the literary world."

Mona felt Shingzwe's words pierce her skin. Her body swelled, the liquid pressure of a big cry mounting inside, ready to burst her chest open. Mona tried to fortify her flesh, arranging a dam around her face by covering it with locks of hair and laughing.

"Oh, Shingzwe! You're such an exquisite poet! Forgive me for behaving this way at your table. I'm very sorry, really, I never should have left my cabin like this. I don't know what I'm doing here. Have you seen the dead fox? I've already found the cadavers of two animals since getting here. Can you believe it? You think I'm the only one who saw them?"

Shingzwe stared into Mona's eyes as she extracted a mentholated Kleenex from her small purse. As Shingzwe reached across the table to offer it to her, Mona noticed a tiny vintage watch dangling from the poet's minuscule wrist. Then she watched as Shingzwe removed a small pencil-like object from her purse, clicked it twice, and sucked on its tip. It was a metallic vape, much more chic than Mona's. She was fascinated.

"You, too?"

"Just apple flavoring." Shingzwe smiled, then kissed the vape with her thin lips. "I started using it to relieve foot pain. Certain shoe styles are agonizing for me to wear. But I don't want to have to wear sneakers all the time. Sneakers can be cute, of course, but they're really not for me. My advice for you is: chill out. That's all. It's not easy to be a young woman with talent. What you're seeking will only come with time, but it'll come."

On her way back to her cabin, Mona wrote four short poems for Mathilde's video. She imagined herself wearing the promised Hermès shawl, arranged in a perfect V across her shoulders, Shingzwe-style—not tied around her neck to hide her bruise, a spiraled shape that had now taken on a yellowish color, with hints of purple, like Jupiter's stormy dark spot.

CAFÉ
Le temps c'est un exercise
d'attente, de prémonition
de penser que tu es
et tu n'es pas

ARBRES
le temps c'est
les vagues des arbres
le souffle
du soleil
dans mon visage

NUIT
la nuit c'est mon ocean
le jeu et les lumières
le vertige du labyrinthe

le temps où tu n'est pas
et le temps que tu es
avec moi

Her lines weren't sublime but they felt fresh. And there was something fundamental about them: the air of something too easy, something effortless, stolen, unelaborated. We can never know what true poetry is, Mona reflected, but what makes a piece of writing recognizable as a poem is the feeling that you're getting ripped off. In the era of technocapitalism, Raoul once told her, the sublime no longer exists; poetry, therefore, has to include a feeling of theft, an intuition of a comparison and competition—value itself should be totally accidental. What's vital is to communicate the feeling of having somehow swindled language—that surely *that* couldn't be a poem. If that couldn't be a poem, that's exactly why it was one. She reread her work with pleasure, then typed out the poems on her phone and sent them over WhatsApp to Mathilde, who was waiting for them on the other side of the world. The fourth poem she wrote in French, but translated it immediately. It was about foxes in the forest, who would soon realize their fur was being darkened by a rising tide from which there was no escape.

7.

A young writer named Gemma Grobovick opened the session with an emotive presentation about her childhood as a Russian Jew in Azerbaijan, and what it was like for a Jewish girl to fall in love with German literature and embrace German as the language in which she chose to write. Seated to her right, waiting for his turn to speak, was Klaus Lursson, a Dane about fifty years old, all bones and sinew like Iggy Pop. The Dane was fiddling impatiently with his microphone cord, like he was counting down the minutes until he could be back at the pub. To Gemma's left sat the Colombian writer Marco Guncio, inspecting the audience with long, sweeping looks cast out from under a broad-brimmed hat.

When applause for Gemma died down, Lowena, acting as the moderator for the panel, took up the mic. She asked the audience to jot down any questions they had for Gemma, since they'd be saving the Q&A for the end, so as not to interrupt the flow of ideas on the panel. Lowena was wearing a very thin pink silk blouse. She looked fresh, radiant. She smiled as she stood up.

"On behalf of all of us at the Meeting, it's my pleasure to welcome Marco Guncio, who's just arrived from Colombia. Marco is the author of *Cartagena in Flames*, a book about a time-traveling hacker who ends up on board the ship of the famous pirate Sir Francis Drake. Marco just landed a few hours ago, so we're hoping he'll have a chance to rest after happy hour at Selma's. For those of you who haven't been yet, we have an open mic there every night—it's the official bar of the festival. Happy hour lasts from five to seven. So from all of us here: a warm welcome to Marco!"

Marco submitted to the applause and took the microphone Lowena was handing him. He preferred to speak standing up, while walking around. He had long hair and wore tall cowboy boots and tight black pants cinched with a thick belt. A wide-brimmed black hat completed his pirate look. He extended the microphone cord with a gesture that reminded Mona of the heartthrob singer Luis Miguel.

"I'm Colombian. I come from South America. For those of you who don't know, we have presidents who sound like they're reggaetón singers: Chavez, Lugo, Lula. Dilma, Cristina, Barcelona. Everything disastrous that happens in the rest of the world happened first in South America. Donald Trump is just figuring out how to be a banana republic boss, and that's already our specialty. We have excellent coffee, plenty of vacation spots, and we raise the best soccer players for you to buy up for your European teams. Our Virgin

Mary is Karl Marx, to whom we always appeal whenever we want to show that we're good people: we might be writers, but we're Marxist writers, on the Left, as we should be. And at the same time we try to convince everybody to lend us money because our capitalism 'works' just the same as any other kind. We eat meat every day and haven't yet managed to get our dogs accustomed to a vegan diet. Oh, and one of us controls all Christendom."

The audience responded sympathetically to his political references. Marco paid the applause no mind, instead gazing silently into the distance. It was his personal theatrical touch.

"So you have to realize: being raised in a place like that, agitating for revolution becomes your true calling. Our parents dedicated their lives to instilling in us the importance of subverting the System. They died in droves. But like my little granny from Cartagena used to say, they had something to die for. And when the Yankees—because that's what we called them—when the Yankees flooded the world with their Coca-Cola and their electric appliances in the sixties, our parents and grandparents carried the revolution forward into the tropics, with their beards and cigars. All this by way of saying, as a reminder, that revolution is an essential part of the South American brand. We found it charming, the way that Marxism came back in style in New York, and the way the Occupy encampments spread like a rash through so many cities. Okay, great, they finally figured it out! We, on the other hand: we were wearing those Che Guevara T-shirts before they were cool."

Marco took off his hat, revealing long, wavy brown hair, undulating down from a receding hairline. He tossed the hat into the air—it floated up and then came down to make a perfect landing on the back of his chair. Amazed, the audience redoubled its attentions. Marco went on:

"The question I'd like to propose we take up is this: How do we create collective forms of resistance in the current political landscape? What can we do anymore, besides tweet? Is there some kind of absolute power still out there, ruling over us? Is there still a singular monster worth fighting? And if so, who is that monster, and where is it hiding?"

Marco made his way between the rows of spectators, stopping in the middle of the tent like an evangelical preacher. The audience was rapt. He had them right where he wanted them.

"First of all, we have to accept that our readers are no longer human. That we're all immersed in an immense narrative, the largest representational endeavor in the history of the world: Google. It organizes and indexes everything you've ever done, and catalogs your desires—even the things you still don't know you'll desire. It keeps statistics on your loves and your hates, the various possibilities for your future. The characters, which is to say, the users, are increasing in number every day. And every day, more of them write themselves into the story, each user doing his or her best to sound just like themselves! The genre for these characters is autofiction, playing at *being real*. We're the characters who populate an omniscient novel that indexes and organizes itself for the benefit of its nonhuman readers. These readers are also searching for something real, something much *more* real, more troubling, a search that leads to surveillance and control."

Marco paused to see what effect this last proclamation was having. The audience was eating it up. The intersection between literature and technology was an inevitable and much-desired theme, and nobody knew where it might lead. The literary world still didn't know what to make of the digital frontier, which was why talks with titles like "How to Lose Friends on Facebook" or "Snapchat and Me" were generally well attended. Writers allowed themselves to share candid moments and realizations with each other because computers had put them all on the same level: they were like children stupefied by fabulous new toys. But technology was a talisman of the now, and if a writer couldn't do much more than stumble from one banality to the next, at least he could console himself with the excuse that nobody ever knows how to speak about the present moment.

Mona sighed, letting her head fall to the side to stretch the muscles in her neck. Marco's spiel was a lot better than the last time she'd heard it. All his dramatic soap-star effects were well rehearsed. And that tossed-hat business: Where had he gotten that? The natural flow of skepticism running through the audience's neural pathways had been effectively blocked. And technology wasn't just a Latin American phenomenon, so that was a plus for his presentation. Whenever the topic was technology and the author didn't limit himself to the usual user travails (like summary expulsions from this or that e-commerce site, which invariably led to a customary ring of the technofascism alarm bell), people expected some kind of Asperger's-level performance, as if speaking about technology with authority required the presenter to be some kind of method actor who could vividly convey memories from his life as a machine. Marco had worked hard on this part: he'd dreamed up a whole new lineage for this pirate persona he was inhabiting, a Latin American lineage. And judging by how things were going, it was working.

"So what does my South American mind, steeped in a Marxist education, have to say about all this? If Google is the great novel of our era, and the creator of this new genre of objective realism, then the future of the human novel might be something like a hack, a mechanism of clandestine writing. Allow me to take you with me on a little detour to the Caribbean waters of my beloved Colombia. This isn't going to be about coffee or drugs, but about something even more deeply rooted in the identity of Cartagena, the city where I was born. As you probably know, a lot of pirates ended up in the Caribbean. At the same time Shakespeare was putting on his plays, English sailors entertained themselves by pillaging Spanish galleons on the high seas, stealing everything the Spanish had already looted from America. Sir Francis Drake was one of the most famous among the many pirates to have lived (and died) obsessed with sacking Cartagena. It was the ultimate target: the richest and most luxurious Spanish port, one surrounded by an extraordinary wall, the most extensive fortification in the entire Spanish Empire. The line of defense not only extended for kilometers; it also hid some nasty surprises, like the double line of cannons the Spanish installed along the thickest wall ever to be built in the Western world. Well, not even Francis Drake could pillage Cartagena. The city knew how to defend itself, because in building its defenses it had thought like a pirate. And that's what I'm inviting you to do today: to think like pirates."

When Mona met him at the Hay Festival in Cartagena, Marco was sporting a classic D'Artagnan look, complete with two swords crossed over his back. "Of course you can carry bladed weapons in Cartagena," he boasted. "Where did you think you were, honey? If you couldn't, this wouldn't be Colombia." He twirled his phallic blades overhead. They were standing in the line for one of the headline events of the festival, during which Salman Rushdie would read selections from his latest book. There were tons of people, everyone in a festive mood. Surely the hologram projecting in Marco's mind resembled something along the lines of a rocker pirate à la Keith Richards. But he reminded Mona more of Lima circa 1991, when teenage hipsters in Miraflores tried to emulate the long-haired lead singer from Poison but ended up looking more like Puss in Boots. While they waited to get in, a kid about twelve years old approached Marco and asked if he wrote fantasy novels. Marco said that no, he wasn't a fantasy writer, his mouth slowly curling into a reluctant smile.

They saw each other again on Cuban Night, an event in a local salsa bar that the festival had organized as a tribute to

José Lezama Lima. Everyone came accompanied by their respective "angels," which was what they called their personal Cerberus. Later Mona found out that Marco's angel wasn't one of the ones hired by the festival. Since he was from Cartagena, he'd brought one of his lady friends, a girl he liked to make jealous by flirting with well-known writers. Miguel Ángel, Mona's *ángel*, was a charming and verbose young man who wanted to be a "journalist or essayist." He was taking courses at the Fundación García Márquez and assured Mona that she could count on his full attention—that since he had the honor of being her *ángel*, he wouldn't think of anything else but her, because that was his duty, on the one hand, but also because thinking about her was such a pleasure. Ever since he'd seen her photo on a book jacket, he'd thought: What a gorgeous writer! But he didn't want her to think he was a sexist, no—please!—definitely not, because he had so many female friends and because he, too, wanted to bring down the patriarchy. But it would have been a betrayal of his body, a betrayal of the male sex to which he belonged, he said, gazing into her eyes, not to tell her the truth. She didn't have to worry because he wouldn't leave her for a minute, just as the festival recommended. She'd be safe with him, her Miguel Ángel *ángel*.

After the obligatory salsa dancing with Miguel Ángel, Mona retreated into a glass of whiskey, wearing the expression of a drunk but magnificently composed Mona Lisa, holding her back erect like a princess. Marco was in his element, sashaying around with his salsa partners, surrounded by "honeys," as he called the women he wanted to sleep with. When he noticed that Mona had excused herself from dancing, he became obsessed with rescuing her from the other men, as well as the hired angels. Mona had grown up in an environment where all the straight boys were devotees of Norman Mailer, committed to the belief that "tough guys don't dance." The sudden struggle over who would get her back on the dance floor reactivated her atavistic fantasy of being a traditional Disney princess.

Mona and Marco bailed on the party, catching a taxi into the Colombian night, winding through the dark streets surrounding that open-air museum called Ciudad Antigua. A song by Ricardo Arjona was playing in the cab, and when they recognized it both Mona and Marco started laughing with horror. They exchanged fugitive kisses, and between peals of laughter, Marco sucked on her tongue—a gesture Mona answered with a slight gag as she took leave of her inhibitions, allowing him to feast on her lips.

They got out of the cab at the Hotel Santa Clara, where they were both staying. Mona was glad to be wearing her raincoat as they crossed the lobby, because she could hide behind its raised lapels as they passed in front of a recent Prix Goncourt winner who was there having a drink, his eyes adrift in a drunken stupor. She'd made out with him the night before, in the hotel pool. Almost as soon as they'd stepped into the colonial hotel room, Marco took a long swig of whiskey and got right down to eating her sushi—that was how she referred to her *sancta sanctorum*—taking slow, wet, practically motionless slurps, lifting his head only to get a good look at her labia majora with his bulging antenna eyes, then diving back down for another whiff and more slurp on slurp.

But Marco's prior demonstration of dance floor virtuosity had promised more dynamic enthusiasm. Mona pulled his face in to her, the better to jog his memory. Instead, he pulled away, whispering, "Honey, I like you so much I want to have your scent under my skin." She heard the twang of another Arjona song in the distance. Marco's mouth went slack, perhaps due to the pairing of rough whiskey and smooth sushi. Then he redoubled his attack, using his wide mouth to eat her out like she was a giant marshmallow flower filled with nectar. His mouth was completely full of her now, his tongue shooting down the middle, digging all the way to the bone. Her nipples hardened as he cupped her breasts, moving up to suck each of them like a plum. Mona took note of these details, cutting Marco out of the scene. Bare and defenseless, wearing just his Calvin Klein briefs, Marco's skinny body looked a bit yellow and puerile. Yet there was something repulsive about it that attracted her. She saw herself as from above, looking like a bouquet squished beneath a beast—a splendid contrast. That's when she realized that Marco was whispering to himself, or rather, whispering to her pussy. She couldn't hear what he was saying, but maybe her *chucha* could. The whispered words worked like a charm on her— whatever it was, Mona didn't take long to cum, finishing almost in spite of herself. She let out a long sigh and looked down at him, still whispering to her pussy. She decided to take advantage of the situation by pretending to be asleep, or passed out, emulating a delicious detail she'd heard about Isabel Preysler, who supposedly drove men crazy that way: the first time she got any of them in bed, Isabel would always pretend to faint after her *petite mort*, right in the middle of the action. Her little boudoir trick drove all the guys nuts and guaranteed total conquest over the author of *The Perpetual Orgy*.

Mona heard Marco say, "You owe me one, honey." She emitted a dry snore by way of reply. But Marco wasn't ready to give up. He put some music on his phone and started kissing her feet, patiently awaiting her return to consciousness. He poured himself another glass of whiskey and returned to his position at her cooch, reciting Borges's "Poema conjetural": "*Finally I encounter / my South American destiny.*" Mona tried snoring at regular intervals. She waited for Marco to curl up beside her and fall asleep, so she could slip out of the room. At last, lying there unconscious, he looked like a golden god, a Latin American Jim Morrison (but not quite, babe), just on the cusp of going to seed.

When the Q&A was over, Marco intercepted her.

"Hey, hey. Were you gonna leave without saying hi? I just got here and didn't see you at breakfast. I haven't heard a peep from you since the Hay Festival. How have you been, Mona? Tell me everything. You know you can trust me."

"There's not much to tell. I'm here. I'm great. Good to see you, Marco. I need a drink."

"Hang on, I'll bring you one! Wait here."

Marco disappeared into the fog of people. After a few minutes he returned with two glasses and an attitude meant to make it seem like they'd never left off sharing their most intimate thoughts.

"So, yeah, I came because it's Sweden, and I'd never been to Scandinavia before. And you know, if there's only one sure thing, something you know for sure, it's that you just never know what might happen."

Mona's thoughts turned to the civilian population, the non-writers, subjected daily to an implacable and aggressive journalistic regimen of clichés and false paradoxes exactly like the ones Marco used. What was he doing at the Basske-Wortz Meeting? He might be an interesting thinker, he might even have some good ideas—but he wasn't a good writer. Marco wasn't one of the genuine heretics, the lucid and wary ones, hiding out among the general population with pencils clenched between their teeth like knives. In the mornings you could hear the deaf howl of that dispersed regiment as they trooped in to their day jobs, half-written novels disguised among the calendars and documents on their tablets and laptops, some of them revising what they'd feverishly written during the night, their eyes blurring into paste as they stared at the word-processing apps on their phones. Sometimes they didn't even need to write; it was enough to dream about writing, to feel life expand and organize into balanced paragraphs, to feel the transformative edge of literature as it structured their lives with the completion of each chapter. They were able to read the minds of others in mirrors of shimmering onyx, and then decant them, molten, into the exquisite mold of a pair of sentences. Marco was not, and had never been, one of them. He couldn't win the prize; the only Latin American really in the running was Mona.

"I don't know, Marco. It must be the jet lag. We're still on different time zones. It's like you're talking at me from thousands of miles away."

The Colombian lowered his voice and grabbed Mona's shoulder—Marco liked to fabricate these moments of intensity.

"The Basske-Wortz. Mona. Do you realize what it means for us to be here? That we're the only Latin Americans? The Swedish Academy—you think they pay no attention to what happens here?"

Mona burst out laughing.

"Marco, do you have any idea how far you are from getting the Nobel Prize? Do you have any idea of how infinitely more likely it would be for a striped unicorn to fall from the sky and kill you? Seriously."

"I was kidding." Marco sipped his drink and gave Mona his best mischievous grin. "But at the same time, you know what? I'm not kidding. I'm dead serious. But I'm saying it for you. Because I know writing is your life. And because you never know, things change all the time. And the only one sure thing—"

"Is that nothing's a sure thing. You already said that, Marco."

"But doesn't it seem like things have changed?"

"What things? And changed in what sense?" Mona's eyes darted around the perimeter of the tent, searching for the Alpine nonfictionalist. No sign of him.

"Well, it used to be that you had to take a leftist position, for example. The culture demanded it. It was the dictatorship of pens and guns, and communism was the aristocracy of the intellectuals. Look at Borges, who shook hands with Pinochet or the dictator of Argentina or whoever it was, I don't remember, and then they'd never give it to him. The Nobel, I mean. And then there's Neruda, who writes his *Nixonicide*, and they give it to him no problem. So there you go: whenever there was a communist in the running, that's who always won."

Mona blinked twice. Marco was a close talker.

"My god, it's been ages since I thought about *Nixonicide*. One of the worst poems of the century. But you don't think they gave Neruda the Nobel just for that, do you?"

"What I'm saying is that the winds of culture have changed entirely. Now that leftist culture is mainstream, it means absolutely nothing. Think about it: What does it mean to be a leftist? Eating vegan? Marching against the banks and then posting about it online with your iPad? The only truly untenable position is to be a militant member of the KKK, or to declare you're a proud homophobe. Capitalism has completely devoured the Left to the point where it no longer has a hold on the very thing that made up its capital: the noble causes. Now the Left is just a more reactionary form of

112

common sense. It has nothing to do with critical thought. It's a groupthink party for people who consider themselves to be good people and feel morally superior to everyone else. The only thing they have in common with the old-guard Left is the will to mete out justice to anyone who goes astray—like Che, when he shot all those deserters in Bolivia. It's a groupthink party"—Marco appeared to enjoy this phrase he'd coined—"which is why I'm telling you: it's almost better not to let yourself be tainted by any of that 'white' Left stuff, because the truly silenced in today's intellectual discourse are those on the Right. For example, to go back to what I was saying before, now they go and give it to Vargas Llosa, an intellectual from the globalized neoliberal right wing, and . . ."

Mona was only paying sporadic attention to Marco's voice as her eyes followed the other writers, chatting as they filed out of the tent. There was no sign of Sven or his lovely lamb jacket.

"Okay, Marco, I think I see where you're going with all this. You're trying to tell me that now the Academy sympathizes with people from the minority you think *I* belong to, the Right, and so now there's a chance for me. And for you, too, right? That's what you're trying to say, isn't it? And that as South Americans we've racked up a bunch of minority points to boot. So now it will be easier for us."

"Oh, honey, I'd never call you a right-winger. Not to anybody. Everyone from Latin America is on the Left. It's just a question of branding. All I ask is that you don't accuse me of phallocentrism—because then I'd have to admit you're right!"

Marco laughed hard at his own joke and then readjusted his pants in the region just below his belt buckle, reorganizing his package. Since Mona's appreciation wasn't immediately forthcoming, he went on:

"You know me, Mona. I'm just an observer. I call it like I see it. Anyway, I think they'll give the Nobel to some kind of AI sooner than they'd give it to either of us." Marco lowered his voice: "There are already teams working on it."

Marco had saddled his hobbyhorse and galloped back to his tech-world watchtower.

"Marco, you can't stop there. Say more. You think there's some kind of imminent literary singularity in the offing, don't you?"

"Not exactly. I sort of have this beef with Ray Kurzweil. I don't know if you've followed it on LitHub—I'll send you the links—but I don't agree with the date he gives as an estimate for the singularity: 2048, the year when computers will be able to reproduce themselves. I figured you knew about all this. In fact, I was thrilled when I saw your name on the Meeting program, not just because I'd get to see you again, but because I figured you'd be up-to-date on everything. Living in Palo Alto, the beating heart of Silicon Valley, with Stanford and all that. Look, I don't want to say so publicly, but they've contacted me. For an experiment. It's already generating some controversy. We're going to be working on a form of literary AI, a sort of noncreative writing. Artificial intelligence functions mainly through feedback loops—it behaves in a way very similar to what humans call *obsession*. People can take psychiatric medications to break out of their obsessive loops, but AI can't exit recursive functions voluntarily. Sort of like how writers get stuck with certain styles."

"And what sort of styles can AI imitate?"

"The whole Thomas Bernhard thing fits them pretty well, for one: long paragraphs that hammer away at the same thing over and over. Anyone who reads too much of it in one go starts to lose their mind, I think. That's why it's funny that Thomas Bernhard has so many imitators in Latin America— unbelievable, really. Whenever somebody gets depressed, you know, it's like they have an internal sensor that tells them: 'Do your Thomas Bernhard imitation. It'll be great: you'll see. It'll be "literary" and give everyone the impression that you're actually saying something important.' But when you get down to specifics, there's still a lot of confusion about AI. Some people say that it's just another version of the monkeys writing *Hamlet* or whatever. But of course they forget that in order for those monkeys to turn out Shakespeare, you have to stipulate an infinite number of them working for eternity—"

"Marco, if they invited you to participate, it's most likely because they want you to be one of their monkeys—right?"

Marco grabbed her by the shoulders. "Hey, why don't we go relax a little? You're all . . . *tense*. Did you realize that? Check out these knots in your back. Are your chakras blocked or what? Want me to do a little reiki on you?"

"Enough, Marco, let go of me."

"Look at what a lucky lady you are. I just traveled twenty hours to get here, and now here I am, fresh as a crisp leaf of kale, ready to give you a little curative massage—and I'm the one who just got off a plane! I should be the one getting the massage!"

Marco let his gaze run across the placid landscape of their provincial retreat and took a deep breath of fresh Swedish air.

"Look, it wouldn't be so bad if they gave you two hundred thousand euros just to say nice things about the place and all the amazing people who put on the festival," he said. "It's really incredible. You know that one of them translates Cervantes into Swedish? I think I'd accept the Basske-Wortz just so that I *could* go around saying nice things about this place. And have the whole world hear me. That's the most important part. Anyway, have you read anything by that Icelandic poet? I know he's hiding out in his cabin, so I haven't seen him yet. I haven't been able to find much of his work online, but I've heard a lot about him."

Mona caught sight of Gemma, the Azerbaijani-German writer, drinking a glass of water by herself, at some distance from the post-session chitchat. She took Marco by the arm and dragged him over to Gemma. The two of them cheerfully congratulated one another on their respective talks. Marco watched as the two women spoke to one another, smiling with ease. Gemma was a redhead, pretty beyond a doubt. And Marco generally did well with white girls—it was Latinas who tortured him. The day's sessions had come to a close and it was getting to be late afternoon—a great time to go see the lake.

The trail descended down a gentle hill and through a pasture of wild grass. The yellow flowers shimmered through Sweden's interminable summer haze. Along the way they met Hava and Chrystos, who were coming up the path on the way back from the lake.

Hava was scandalized that Mona hadn't heard her contribution to the open mic night at Selma's—the pub was named after Selma Lagerlöf—because she'd dedicated it to her. Mona expressed her regrets and offered a contrite excuse: she'd totally passed out in her cabin. Hava was looking a bit worse for wear, as though a few hours of sleep and a day without makeup had transformed her back into a run-of-the-mill, dirty-haired, down-at-heel literary slob in rumpled house clothes. These were, in fact, her only clothes, since Air Berlin had lost her luggage when she connected at Frankfurt.

"Bunch of anti-Semites!" Mona remarked, offering to lend Hava something to wear. The Israeli smirked, then accepted her offer with a feigned sob. Just then, Marco and Gemma joined the circle in shock. The cause, it seemed, was Akto: he was barreling toward them with a towel under his arm, wearing a white sweatshirt and nothing below it but his Greco-Roman sandals. He greeted the group with his usual cordiality:

"Hi, I'm Akto. I started out as a translator from Ancient Greek and Latin, and then from Swedish and Finnish, but recently I decided to write fiction."

Gemma lurched as Akto's renegade dong came closer. She took refuge behind Marco, who held out his arm in a protective gesture. Mona had gotten used to sharing space with Akto's liberated Nordic phallus and gleefully invited him down to the lake with them. She'd already decided she liked him—plus, she adored dead languages. It was logical that Akto, so immersed in the Hellenic world of two-thousand-odd years ago, would experience a few glitches whenever he teleported his mind to the present. On their way down to the lake, they talked about the magic of Greek prepositions—the true motor of the language—and Akto recited a poem by Horace, to Mona's delight.

"You want to hear T. S. Eliot in Greek? Sometimes I translate contemporary poets to Ancient Greek, just to see how they sound."

With the joy of an adventurous child, Akto then went on to recite Bob Dylan's "Blowin' in the Wind" in Latin:

Responsum est, mi amice, in vento flante exsurgebat,
Responsum est in vento flante exsurgebat

Mona laughed, enchanted. Paradise was a Swedish lake adorned with a gentle sun, white and cottony, a distant and elegant star that didn't want to punish all life beneath it. An authentic prime mover, not moving or being moved, which does not love and is not loved, as Aristotle defined his idea of the creator hovering beyond his creation. It ordered all life. Such harmony as was found below could only exist in conjunction with its solar abyss, but nothing could make it feel vulnerable, nothing could cause it anxiety or provoke its fury. No, it couldn't be moved—like Akto's dick, dangling undaunted by the world. By contrast, the Lord of Armies, the one who'd interested her so much during her studies of the Hebrew Bible, was clearly a creature of the desert who made much of his torrid personality.

Akto said goodbye, and Mona felt a cold hand slide around her waist.

"I have to learn to take pointers from you," Gemma whispered in her ear, now taking her by the arm. "Anyone who knew enough to skip that little improvised lecture Hava gave at open mic night is someone who understands many things. On top of that, she'd dedicated it to you. In other words, you were the muse of our torture."

"Really?"

Mona stared back at Gemma, hanging from her arm. She had the appeal of a dangerous redhead, the kind of strawberry blonde who produced a certain fascination in Mona— the sort of woman who knows how to sway between apparent calm and the sudden and surprising aggression that was the true shape of her personality. It was pretty uncommon to bad-mouth another writer so early into a conference. Probably, Mona figured, this absence of social graces had its origins in a studied millennial pose Gemma was trying to strike. But then again, perhaps it *wasn't* so early in the conference anymore—maybe time was flying, and with so much Valium in her system Mona hadn't noticed, lodged in her own temporal snail shell, having fallen from the nibbled leaf of reality.

Gemma told Mona she looked like Asia Argento without the tattoos. Or did she have tattoos? Mona was pretty well covered up in her raincoat, with the handkerchief still wrapped around her neck. No, she told Gemma, she restricted herself to electronic ink.

"I mean, I love your look as is—the vintage raincoat makes you look like you stepped off the set of an eighties porno," Gemma assured her as she lit a Marlboro.

Mona complimented Gemma on her excellent makeup. She had great technique with her contour and complemented it well with her shading: gray and blue, with extensive application of black eyeliner that made her almond-shaped blue eyes pop. Gemma resumed her shit-talking:

"God. I can't even begin to explain that open mic to you. My great-grandparents didn't die in a concentration camp for me to have to listen to shit like that. I'm telling you: it made me ashamed to be Jewish. I'm so sick of everything people say in the name of the Jews, the way they take our views for granted, our positions. Just take one look at the Israeli-Palestinian conflict and you realize there's fascists on both sides of every issue. It's all too much."

Farther down the beach, Akto had taken off his sweatshirt and waded into the water, singing an emphatic marching tune with Greek alexandrine verses.

"That guy's amazing, the gem of the entire Meeting," Mona said.

Gemma's mouth immediately exchanged its irritated expression for a smile. Then Marco approached.

"Let's get in the water. Whattaya say, girls?"

Marco made a big show of taking off his backpack and leather jacket, tossing them onto the sand before peeling off his clothes, watching the two women throughout the procedure. Mona let herself collapse onto the sand, as though a bolt of lightning had just split her head open. Flattened on the ground, she stretched her stiff neck and legs.

"Good call, Mona. You need to relax! That's what I like to see. All right, enjoy the beach. I'm gonna take a dip and try to get rid of that airplane vibe. I'll be right back. Make yourselves comfortable! There's nothing like sprawling in the sand to lift your spirits."

Marco faced the shore, still in his T-shirt and black briefs.

"His name's Marco, right? You know him from the South American circuit?"

"Yeah, but not very well."

"Hey, would you happen to have some more of that lipstick on you? It's such a deep purple—almost grape, but with a touch of fresh blood. It looks great on you. Can I try some on?"

Mona handed her the tube of lipstick. Gemma took out a compact and studied a beauty mark on her face. She ran the lipstick across the back of her hand, smeared it off, and only then brought it to her lips.

"See what I mean? You know what you're doing. Chanel Rouge. It's exactly the kind of thing I'd never expect to wear just to hang out by a lake, and you even brought it with you. You're my idol. I want to be like you when I grow up."

"Well, you're doing pretty well already, don't you think?" Mona took a deep hit off her vape, allowing the smoke to exit her body in one long, smooth exhalation. Bony Marco, in his little black briefs, moved closer to the water's edge. He got to where the water was lapping the sand and then took little hops back from the tiny waves. He backed up to get a running start and finally sprinted full-speed into the tide. He stopped almost as soon as he hit the water, remained immobile for a few seconds, then ran back out the way he came.

"You asked if I knew him? There. That's all you need to know about him."

"Nothing like frigid water for a man's ego."

As Marco stood beside the lake, freezing in as manly a manner as possible, something in the distance caught Mona's eye. Parallel to the horizon, she thought she could see lights in the sky. In the moment she counted three glimmering spots over the water, but later she realized there had been many more, like there were boats made of mirrors floating out there, their slanted surfaces reflecting the sun. Momentarily blinded, Mona barely registered the dark black shape entering her peripheral vision, advancing slowly over the sand.

It was Lena Bactreau, coming toward them with towels. Mona covered her face with her arm, accidentally flinging sand into her hair. Then she started covering her entire body with sand, until she looked like a breaded cutlet. Gemma watched her do it, unnerved.

"Hi, Lena, how's it going? This is Gemma. She's a monster, too."

"Hello, Mona—hello, Gemma. Great talk, by the way. I found it very interesting."

"Hi, Lena, and thanks."

"Are you getting in the water, Lena? You can sit with us and play makeover if you want."

"What's this about me being a monster?" Gemma was still on alert. She hadn't understood the reference and didn't want them to make fun of her without being in on the joke.

"Lena's a student of Kali, the Hindu goddess of thugs. Kali was the first to ever use lipstick: she spread red blood around her mouth so that everyone would know she was coming to devour the enemy. She also wore necklaces made of her victims' skulls. Kali was the biggest it-girl of all antiquity, as her legacy today attests."

Lena emitted a series of guttural grunts: her laugh.

"I see you've done some research, Mona. Well done. Maybe that's what I'll speak about tomorrow. At the open mic. Nice to meet you, Gemma."

Lena continued on down the beach. Gemma stretched out on the sand, lying on her side and smoking a cigarette.

"Hey, have you ever had a three-way?"

"I'm sorry?"

"With Marco?"

"You think we're together?"

"Here." Gemma fished in her bag and handed Mona a tiny jar of eye cream. "Here, some of your eyeliner's running."

Stationed at the edge of the scene, Lena Bactreau contemplated the open water. When Akto emerged from the lake, Lena zeroed in on him, handing him a towel to dry himself off.

And, just then, Mona saw three heads rise up from the water, haloed in hair. It was three men, immobile underwater, allowing only their heads to surface for air. They must have been there the entire time, because Mona hadn't seen them arrive. She must have had a look of horror on her face, because Gemma touched her arm in an attempt to reassure her.

"Hasn't anyone told you about them? They wander around the forests here. But don't try to talk to them: they won't speak to anyone. It's rare for them to get this close. Whenever I see them . . . it's like none of the rest of us even exist for them. But if we don't exist for them, how come they're always hanging around us? I don't get it."

Mona let her eyes drift down to her bare feet on the coarse sand, then looked back up at the men in the lake. Now she counted seven immobile heads, their blond hair darkened by the water.

8.

The tent was packed to capacity. With an unkempt beard growing in, wrapped in a leather jacket decorated with a billiard eight ball, reading from his prepared notes, Philippe Laval let his gaze fall solemnly over the world.

"Because I'm in here," Philippe said, gesturing to his thorax. "And it's from in here that I write. I have nothing but miseries to recount. My subject is shamelessness and the pain of being, and of contemplating, and of hearing this voice and not being able to do anything to stop it. I write, dreaming that someday I'll be able to silence it. I write and I dream, and everything falls into a deafening silence that can't be escaped or altered, and there's no other choice but to write."

The audience listened in silence as Philippe continued. There was something vaguely familiar about Philippe's talk, but Mona couldn't put her finger on what it was. His delivery gave no indication of where he expected people to laugh. There were no jokes parceled out like little caramels for the audience to suck on. Some of the writers had already slipped out of the tent, but Mona didn't bother to work out which ones. She stayed put, clutching her notebook as if she'd collapse if she relaxed her grip. Philippe's talk was in the confessional-psychological mode, very much in vogue. The strange thing was that his confession had to do with admitting to writing, that is, the act itself, as though he weren't speaking to a packed house of other writers. It was like trying to sell Bibles to a book club full of nuns. The implicit premise of a festival like this—where writers are meant to give talks to other writers, and where the presence of civilians is limited at best—is to suppose that the attendees are gathered to converse and debate. But in Philippe's jeremiad, there was nothing to debate. It gave the whole performance an air of mystery, as if he were really stripping bare his soul.

Mona closed her eyes, letting the words wash over her like music. It was her method of escaping into herself, a skill that allowed her to remain affiliated to a university, and thanks to which there was no such thing as an unproductive class or lecture. It was how she started writing: she burrowed down into a hole inside herself until she could look back up at the world with a sense of fascination. Her technique was based on the idea that, with the right equalization, anything could be turned into music or else completely negated. It allowed Mona to wander through a space in which things seemed to take turns obscuring and illuminating one another.

Everything anyone said unfolded in her mind like she was reading a novel, with every detail advancing toward an occult meaning to be untangled. She started focusing on the rhythm of the words, finding the poetic meter hidden inside sentences, the subterranean rhythms of whatever she was listening to. And now, without meaning to, she laughed. On the other side of the speakers' platform, the writer from Algeria smiled.

How had it taken her so long to realize it? Philippe Laval was reciting entire passages from *Malone Dies* in his own strange English translation. The latest sensation in French literature was standing there ripping off Samuel Beckett. What fit of desperation had compelled him to plagiarize entire paragraphs? Did he really think that nobody else in a group composed completely of writers was going to notice?

Maybe it was some kind of postmodern gesture, a piece of performance art. Philippe continued reading without lifting his eyes from his notes. He'd omitted citing his source, of course, but he'd also, at least so far, omitted the cliché. The only thing that would have made his theft an unacceptable vulgarity was serving up the pop refrain that everybody knew: try, fail, fail again, etc., etc. Mona felt a chill as the phrase *fail better* crossed her mind. After all, Beckett, like Heidegger, was basically a self-help writer for the intellectual class—and today's intellectuals seemed ready to ingest mountains of far more solid and pernicious excrement.

The idea that the Author was well and truly dead, that there could be no more valid interpretation of texts, that everything must mean something different depending on who's doing the reading—it was the intellectual justification for the present crisis of meaning in the #fakenews media and in democracy more generally. Pretending that the nonsense intellectuals discussed among themselves remained limited to their caste, a rarified discourse that would never spill over into the rest of the world—it was complete bullshit. The ivory tower was constantly being looted.

When he finished his reading, Philippe made for the side exit, rolling a cigarette as he went. Mona followed him and, after glancing around to be sure that nobody else could hear, she snatched the cigarette out of his hand.

"*Malone. Malone meurt.*"

Philippe flipped open a benzene Zippo with a skull engraved into it and lit what was now Mona's cigarette. He held her gaze with a radiant expression, coming to life for the first time since they'd met. It was like he'd been awakened from his lethargy and was only now fully present, an unexpected ripple in the surface of his world having charged him with adrenaline.

"*Hélas.* Are you going to tell on me? Give me up to the festival authorities? We've already been introduced, but now we're finally getting to know each other."

"I won't tell anyone. Frankly, I don't give a fuck."

"Well, if you squeal on me, they won't give me the prize. It's as simple as that. They don't enjoy controversies, and there's already been enough drama in the Academy. And these guys, the people who organize the Meeting, are capital-L literature people. Anyway, it's fine, I'm used to being poor. In Paris, you're always poor. I don't deserve the prize and they'd never give it to me anyway, which is probably a blessing in disguise. I'm looking forward to your presentation. I assume that you're not going to make a pathetic spectacle of yourself like I did, even if no one else noticed. I read that your talk is about something to do with the Amazon? I'm very interested in the Amazon. Although I've never been to South America."

"I copied the entire thing out of a tourist guide. What do you think of that?"

Philippe laughed, his tobacco-stained teeth chewing air.

"You just don't get it, do you? Why anyone would do something like that."

"Look, just tell me one thing: How could it ever have seemed like a good idea? Beckett is such a well-known writer. Too well-known. Did you really think that nobody would notice?"

"Let's go to the party at the pub. It's starting now, since today's presentations are over. I'll tell you something on the way—and you'll realize how much I appreciate you, because it's something I wouldn't tell anyone else. I sort of liked how they put me on the schedule as a keynote, a big finale to the day's events. And now everyone's leaving here depressed after hearing me. Or at least disappointed. With that in mind, I probably won't bother showing up at another one of these things for another five years at least. That's all literary festivals are good for: the memory of them is so repulsive, and you end up so disgusted by the writing 'community' that you have no choice but to stay home and write. *Seul contre tous*. It's the only thing that justifies the existence of these festivals."

Philippe spoke with vigor, demonstrating an energy that no one could have expected after watching his talk. He seemed transformed, as if the man who lived inside this hollow shell of a writer had decided to come out to play. Attracted by his freshly circulating blood, a mosquito landed on Philippe's cheek. Mona squinted to observe it more carefully. She didn't have great eyesight, but she was never mistaken when it came to identifying insects: it was definitely a mosquito. She slapped Philippe in the face.

He brought a hand to his reddened cheek.

"It's nothing—you just had a mosquito on your face. Please continue."

Philippe had frozen in place, simply beaming.

"That's something a character of mine might say. And to tell you the truth, recognizing *Malone* is something one of my characters would have done, too. Are you real? Do you always go around slapping people you've just met?"

"I come from the jungle and have been a guerrilla in the war against the mosquitoes since the day I was born. I advocate total extermination. No prisoners."

Together they hiked up the hill to Selma's. They walked

slowly, as if moving through a dream where other people appear diffuse, washed out by the rain. Maybe Philippe was right: nobody got near them, as though his talk had cloaked him in invisibility for a few hours. Perhaps, from his point of view, it was a liberation—from other people's stares, so full of desires, so full of questions that demanded some kind of response.

But then again, Mona said, maybe the talk hadn't gone the way he'd expected. Maybe, in the context of an international literary festival, the sort of existential mortification he'd tried to convey was merely read as something very *French*. Maybe, Mona ventured, intellectualizing one's suffering was just the regional brand, in the same way that Marco signaled his Latin American bona fides by peppering his speech with references to Che Guevara and Luis Miguel, or the way Abdollah branded himself a Proud Muslim Invader. The ways that each of them appropriated their own local colors and used them as the backdrop for playing their parts in the theatrical literary market: these were just the modern tools of the trade, weapons in the battle royale of "world lit." Perhaps, by placing his personal pathos front and center, Philippe was being consistent with his ethnic traits. She couldn't be sure, but it was a possibility.

"I agree, it's quite possible. I'll have to think more about it. I'm interested in the total destruction of every expectation. It's my métier. I don't know if that's also something you'd call 'very French.' And I'm not so sure that my personal apocalypse is just a product, like a type of cheese. But it's an interesting theory . . ." Philippe cleared his throat. "In fact, I'm not sure which is more humiliating: if it's just something French, or if it's not French at all."

At Selma's the party was just getting started, but the writers' destruction had accelerated along an exponential curve. Leaning against the bar, some drunk Swedes and Russians were giving encouraging cheers to Carmina, who was dancing on a table, teetering in her red high heels. The Algerian writer and the other Arabs applauded her from below, totally in their element. Carmina was dancing to Prince's "1999."

The back of the pub turned out to have a dance floor with light-up tiles. The Latvian poet was leading a short train with three Swedish women and Seija, a marvelous Finn who looked like a gigantic Marilyn Monroe. From the moment he crossed the threshold with Mona, Philippe had returned to his lugubrious, hunched-over posture, curving into himself like a question mark. He appeared newly afflicted in the midst of that vivid human tableau, as if the embarrassing behavior of drunk people having fun were somehow tinged with his own personal shame. It looked like he'd even lost more hair since arriving at the Meeting. Maybe that would inspire him to write, too.

When Luis Miguel's "Será que no me amas" started playing, Marco felt the call of the jungle and started spinning like a top. He tried giving a dance lesson to Katja, one of the

Swedish writers, while Gemma and Martje, a writer from the Netherlands, did the Robot. On the edge of the illuminated dance floor, Lena and Akto had combined to form a distinctive eight-armed beast, gorging itself on its own kisses. Philippe made straight for the bar, and Mona for the bathroom.

She found the Korean writer rinsing her hands at the sink. Mona hadn't exchanged a word with her since the van ride. She didn't even know her name. On this occasion, the Korean lady had swapped her knitting bag for a chic little nightclub-style clutch. She was examining her eye, face mere centimeters from the mirror.

"Hello!" she chirped, without looking at Mona.

"Hi!"

As Mona entered one of the stalls, the Korean headed for the exit, nearly running smack into Philippe when she opened the door.

"Mona? Can I have a word with you?"

"Philippe! The men's room is next door."

Mona threw the lock on her stall and pulled out her phone. There were new clues about what had happened to Sandrita. A woman who worked in a nearby meatpacking plant said she remembered that on the night of the girl's disappearance she'd seen her walking with a man, and then getting into a car. But that was all. Nothing to do but wait. Unread messages from Antonio and Franco. Mathilde adored her poems. Mona searched for more news about

Sandrita but the intervening three minutes had yielded no new information. Nothing to do but wait. She pocketed her phone and left the stall. Standing at the sink, right where she'd left the Korean writer, was Philippe, staring at himself in the mirror with an absent expression.

"WTF," Mona said.

"Nothing, it's nothing, it's just . . . *Nothing is more real than nothing*," Philippe said, turning toward her. He'd pulled down his pants and was absentmindedly tugging on his dick. Leaning back against the bathroom counter, he jerked off indolently in Mona's direction. He was staring at her with a sad smile, like an exhibitionist version of the Joker.

"Do me a favor and put that away. You'll catch cold."

Mona stampeded out of the bathroom. She didn't feel disgust or embarrassment. What disturbed her the most was the look on Philippe's sweaty face, that broken doll's smile, and the way the amusing person who'd walked her to the bar had disappeared once more. Her feminist values weren't located in her brain stem, so she never experienced any visceral reactions in their name—but she couldn't stand to be in the same place as that Beckettian cock for a second longer. Philippe's branding was stale. The lecherous Frenchman thing was beyond cliché—nobody could outdo DSK. Mona went straight to the bar, where various Swedes sat leaning over the soft fizz of their beers. She remembered something her editor Giovanni Boyd once said to her: all literature is masturbatory or copulative. Philippe, apparently, had made his choice. Most likely, his intent was not to seduce her or even touch her. Maybe all he needed from her was rejection: to fail, fail again, fail better. On the jukebox, New Order's "Age of Consent" was in its death throes; "Girl U Want" by Devo took over.

She laughed to herself, and since she was standing at a bar, her solitary laughter functioned as a kind of greeting to everyone else. Chrystos moved to intercept her.

"They're about to start the open mic, and everyone keeps telling me about a video of you singing bossa nova. They all want you to sing. Please, you have to. I can't stand to hear another spoken-word 'reflection on the current era.'" Chrystos rolled his eyes.

"You know what? I think your argument has been disproven, Chrystos. It's not that there are no more literary personalities in our era: it's just that now they come to places like these thinking they're writers and end up leaving as characters. The festivals are the real novels!"

Mona ordered another whiskey and popped the liquor-coated ice cube from her first drink into her mouth. She was Peruvian, but it didn't matter what she sang: bossa, tango, *valsecito*, or *chacarera*. Peru, Argentina, Brazil: what difference did it make to the gringos? When they saw her wearing a Peruvian soccer shirt, they cheered for Argentina because they couldn't tell the difference between logos and had never heard of River Plate. When they saw her out dancing in New York, they spoke to her in Portuguese. And below the Amazon—which is to say, in South America's own subconscious—everything was just a maze of tunnels and traps and thoughts held captive in Quechua, a language that had crystallized a grammar much closer to German than to any of the Romance languages, those orchids brought in from Latium. The South was the largest and most loosely defined region in the world.

Mona downed her drink and marched to the stage. Behind her, Chrystos was making wild hand gestures at the sound guy to alert him of the upcoming performance. As soon as the ongoing round of songs was over—because Selma's functioned like a Latin American wedding, with rounds of dancing followed by courses of food and music—it would be Mona's turn to sing.

"You want to run to the bathroom to touch up your makeup? No wait, you look perfect already," Chrystos assured her.

Pas du tout, Mona thought, blowing Chrystos a kiss before retracing the contours of her mouth in blood red. She didn't need a mirror. She was on another plane, her anesthetized brain licking itself like a cat in her mental salon. She hummed the first song that came to mind: "Vete de mí," an exquisite bolero by a tango duo, the brothers Homero and Virgilio Expósito, the Mick Jagger and Keith Richards of quintessential Latin American syncretism.

But she changed her mind. It was too baroque, too contorted. It lacked the razzle-dazzle required to engage the masses, no matter how drunk they were. Mona's mind went blank, and she sang with eyes closed, as if she were alone.

The words came from deep down, and as she sang she gazed into the distance, her neck languidly stretched out to project her song beyond the audience and into the blackness of night.

Perdida, me ha llamado la gente
Sin saber que he sufrido con desesperación.

She loved boleros: they transported her to her own personal sound booth, which allowed her to sing a cappella with a full voice that was sufficient all on its own, like she were her own orchestra. When she stopped singing, she opened her eyes.

All movement in Selma's bar had ceased. The director of the festival, Eino Eleino, started up a slow, loud clap— either he was doing the American slow-clap of appreciation or he was completely drunk. Mona thanked him by putting a hand to her heart, then reached for the glass of water that Chrystos was holding out to her. Marco appeared from behind Chrystos, thrusting a little yellow and white flower in her face: a frangipani he'd taken from one of the table arrangements.

"Put it behind your ear, *flor de canela.*"

He planted a kiss on her cheek and, taking her by the waist, steered her smoothly away, as if they were dancing salsa. In a matter of seconds, however, Marco had commandeered the microphone to put on his own act. Mona felt her phone buzz and reluctantly took it out. She'd forgotten to turn it off. She sat down by a far wall. The news was being reported by all the big Lima newspapers: Sandrita had been found on the banks of the Rímac River, with signs of having been strangled and gang-raped. She'd been dragged through the weeds, and her wounds indicated the involvement of more than one person. The press had started to call her the Ophelia of the Rímac.

"Mona, you want to do an encore? Or a duet with Marco? Mona, are you okay?"

She clutched her throat. It was pulsating like a reptile's. She could barely breathe. Her eyes filled with tears.

She reached for Chrystos's knee. Distracted, he handed her a flask of whiskey. She felt a weight on her, like someone holding her down. Eyes closed, immobile beneath her aggressor's blows, clay between her fingers. Hate was like an incandescent odor, attempting to break her. Pinioned legs kicking in terror. Her fingernails were useless. It was impossible to defend herself; she was nothing but a ball of flesh and hair. Beaten underwater. How long did bruises last underwater?

"*I see you. You can't escape.*"

The whiskey made its journey through Mona's interior labyrinth, igniting her nervous system with a valiant, passionate, righteous glow. She muscled her way back onstage. She would sing for Sandrita, for that girl and for all the girls who lived and died beyond the river's edge.

Déjame que te cuente, limeña
Déjame que te diga la gloria . . .

The night was hers—she brought the audience to its feet—but Mona felt destroyed, singed inside. Her rapid descent from the stage was misinterpreted as a sudden attack of timidity.

9.

Eino Eleino arrived at the little reception in the spa café, harried by his duties. He was carrying two books under his arm, as well as the Swedish edition of the *Quixote*. Lowena followed close behind, hugging a package to her chest, underneath her notebook. It turned out to be an armful of red and blue jerseys, which she handed to a small group of Russians so that they could distribute them to the other writers.

That morning, Arkadi Sergey Vladimirovich had read some poems in Russian. They were musical, superlative pieces chock-full of winks and Ancient Greek puns—wordplay that forged correspondences between the private lives of the Cyrillic and Greek alphabets. His work made sarcastic allusions to Heraclitus and Parmenides, among other Hellenic philosophers who'd been dead for millennia. Even though the verses were pretty opaque to anyone who didn't speak both Greek and Russian, it was possible to detect which bits were risqué by the complicit tone in which the Russian read his lines, as well as the way he punctuated each phrase, his little blue eyes connecting with the knowing smiles of his gang of disciples, who listened to him with delight. Although she didn't really understand a word of it (her Ancient Greek had gotten rusty over the years), Mona was enchanted by Arkadi's performance: If nothing existed, and if literature were all that was real, then why should we pretend otherwise? Why pretend that we believe in the existence of a shared world if all that exists is literature? That was for civilians, not real writers—this was what Arkadi seemed to be telling her in Russian, the contraband smuggled between his verses. Such pacts founded upon cowardice—the Russian continued, in Mona's internal translation—could only concern the masses, the uninitiated, the servants of some borrowed bourgeois ideal. Arkadi's eyes couldn't find a place to rest in the audience, taking in all that moved and all that remained still, all things animate and inanimate, beyond sky and sea. When he finished, the director of the festival took the floor.

"Dear friends, I want to thank you all for crossing skies and seas, cities and countries, to join us for this very special session of the Meeting. Here, something big unites us, something greater than appreciation, greater than taste: we go together into the silent battle of pen and ink as a united front of comrades and lovers. I cannot in all honesty say that I'm the lover of all of you, because I wouldn't want to tempt the police to start investigating me. But yes, we're comrades! Comrades in ink and letter, comrades and lovers, as in Walt Whitman's *Leaves of Grass*. I sing for you and for us, my comrades in ink! Comrades in ink, united! Let us sing of the life of the pen, the life in words!"

With this little call to arms, the director of the festival inaugurated an event of historic importance in the trajectory of the festival: the annual soccer match between Sweden and the Rest of the World.

The Swedes put on blue jerseys; the Rest of the World was in red. Gemma and Martje were wearing dark shorts that revealed their sturdy all-terrain knees. Akto had likewise condescended to wearing shorts. There among the Swedes was the hot nonfictionalist. Would she brush against him during the game as he blazed by at top speed, in total control of the ball? Or would he shove her "accidentally," the two of them tumbling into the sand together?

Two writers on the Rest of the World team, Fabrizzio and Klaus, revealed themselves to be soccer philosophers. They explained that, the night before, the two of them had devised the perfect strategy for defeating Sweden. They'd play without a goalie, in compact formation: Abdollah would hang back as the last defender. Wearing shorts and socks pulled up to his knees, Abdollah nodded his assent with utter seriousness, warming up in place with little jumps. Martje and Carmina were the flank defenders, while Gemma would be their midfielder. Martje asked why they couldn't just play three up and three back. "This is going to be a quick game of tiki-taka, like the Barça of Pep Guardiola," Fabrizzio explained without hesitation, rhythmically cracking his knuckles as he spoke. Marco, the Colombian, would be a side forward. Chrystos would take the other side, the two of them connected by Klaus, who would lead the midfield. They'd have two captains: Fabrizzio and Klaus would take turns calling the shots, depending on whether the team was playing defense or offense.

Fabrizzio and Klaus held their breath when they saw Lena Bactreau, implacable and enormous, approaching over the sand, her defiant gaze aimed like a fusillade in their direction. She took a seat on the sidelines near the midfield line and declared herself team trainer for the Rest of the World, offering deep-tissue massage to anyone who needed it. Fabrizzio ran over to give her an appreciative hug.

The Italian captain waved the Rest of the World over to join in on the hug, forming a mass of arms and giggles. Philippe, the Frenchman, had refused to put on a jersey, but joined in the collective hug, wishing everyone a good game.

After Sweden's first two goals, the spirit of cooperation among the Rest of the World collapsed. The Italian captain was furious with his Danish counterpart. A friendship forged by nocturnal complicity and a white night's summer bender was in ruins. In accordance with their national lifestyles, the little Italian only thought about defense, while for the Dane, who had the look of a blond proletarian dragged out of a pub, soccer was all about the English fake-out, an attack that consisted of advancing along the sides, passing to the middle, and head-butting forward. Fabrizzio roared like a bear, caged behind the midfield line, crossing it from time to time just to bicker with Klaus as he ricocheted across the field. Whenever someone from his team got near the ball, he howled phrases of encouragement, urging the girls to run harder. Abdollah, for his part, demonstrated that being quick on your feet doesn't preclude being a complete klutz. After the fourth Swedish goal, the Italian captain took Abdollah by the shoulders and assured him, "We can win this, trust me!" He made some player substitutions, which consisted of taking all the girls off the field and replacing them with the men who'd remained on the sidelines: it was up to them to salvage the honor of the Rest of the World. Martje sullenly plopped down next to Lena, saying that Fabrizzio didn't understand that it was just a game. By way of reply, Lena enumerated all the traits that Fabrizzio, in her view, shared with Berlusconi. Emboldened by swelling waves of hatred for the enemy, Fabrizzio caught a pass and dribbled straight downfield, a solitary man in search of his goal, like his Neapolitan god Maradona, charging against the English.

But Sweden was invulnerable. Its strength knew no bounds.

And so it was that Sweden defeated the Rest of the World, for the first time in the history of the Meeting. The Vikings embraced and leaped for joy. The girls, resentful of the captains of the Rest of the World, cheered the Swedish victory while the Swedes took off their jerseys and began to hug and congratulate the Rest of the World on playing a good game.

Both teams partook in euphoric leaping for as long as anyone was snapping photos for posterity.

With the game over, the writers were guided to the lake for celebratory beers. The Nordic victors stripped off their shorts and walked nude to the edge of the glassy lake. Hava and Arkadi imitated them, though they didn't seem to realize they'd just missed the game. Although she'd run quite a bit, and would have been relieved to cool off, Mona was already familiar with the frosty shiver that inhabited the lake, like an animal waiting to nip at human feet. She didn't dream of getting near it. Instead she sat down in the sand to enjoy the view, wrapped in her raincoat and drinking vodka from a beer bottle.

As the alcohol made its way to her brain, flooding the channels between ideas, Mona's thoughts were like an archipelago welcoming the rising seas. Her head hung low, eyes wet with the bleary bright. She pulled a leg behind her head, a yoga pose that she considered unbeatable for the way it reduced her to the sensation of being a throbbing, mute body. She closed her eyes and massaged the back of her neck, returning to the world only when the light of the kind Swedish sun suddenly seemed to blink off. Sven was standing over her. He'd taken off his leather jacket and was sipping a beer, casting his shadow across her.

"Hello, miss. I think you sing better than you play soccer."

His Spanish was surprisingly decent. Mona maintained her position and smiled, inviting him to sit down.

"My name is Sven Olle Siggurdsson. I'm like everything else around here: a native. You're from Peru, right?"

Mona nodded. "I didn't see you sweating it out in a Swedish jersey."

"It was bad enough that you guys lost seven to one. It was clear my country didn't require my services."

"Very kind of you to restrain yourself."

Sven rolled his pants up to his knees. His legs were obscenely perfect. He probably ran marathons.

"Anyway, I'm hurt. I twisted my ankle playing with my dog. Fell right over, somehow. Not really sure what I did."

"And your dog is actually a Norse dragon, I presume."

"I think my body is lucky I'm a writer. It doesn't stand a chance against clumsy mishaps. It's probably punishing me for getting too active. Wouldn't surprise me at all if it were some kind of secret sadist."

Down at the lakeshore, the winning team appeared to be conducting a ritual. Katrina, one of the Swedish writers, and Seija, the giant blond Marilyn, danced around without their jerseys on, undulating their arms like documentary-footage hippies. Then they stripped completely naked and jumped in the lake. Sven hadn't been nominated for the Basske-Wortz; he and Katia and Seija were with Akto in what Mona was mentally calling the Nordic Track. A few yards away, Akto and a few other Scandinavian writers were drinking beer and shouting in the direction of the women in the lake. Katrina and Seija's nude bodies shone with snowy resplendence against the idyllic landscape, like they were off-duty

Valkyries or water nymphs. The sun bathed them in a spectral evening light, disappearing into heavenly white death throes that never seemed to end.

"Lovely view, isn't it?" asked Sven. "Have you tried our national waters?"

"I prefer to watch. It's marvelous: the sun really does seem to bring out the best in all of you. You're aspirational Latinos, you Scandinavians."

"Tell the truth—you're just afraid of freezing if you get in the lake. Where's that hot Latin blood I've heard so much about?"

Mona laughed. Aside from her trench coat, she was wearing a cashmere sweater and her silk scarf, wrapped all the way up to her ears. At the other end of the beach, chatting in a small group, Marco was likewise cloaked for winter, in cap and leather.

"Why don't you tell me, Sven, where your mastery of hot-blooded Spanish comes from?"

"In high school they made us choose a language besides English to learn, and my parents always took us to the Canary Islands on vacation. So Spanish made sense. Later on I took a trip through Mexico and Central America. I even lived awhile in Nicaragua."

"What'd you think?"

"Well, it was . . . pretty dirty, above all else. And hot, of course. But it was great for my Spanish."

"Spanish is bad for the brain."

"How so?"

"There's no rule in Spanish to prevent infinite sentences. Just listen for our subordinate clauses. Or, I should say, listen for us indulging our intrinsic vice for subordinate clauses. There's nothing in the grammar to stop you from subordinating till the end of time, and yet at the same time, it gives you the illusion that you're articulating a well-formed sentence. It's baked into the language, you can find it in Cervantes. In fact, Spanish invites you to subordinate all things to other things, in an interminable wave of subordination—because Spanish has a concept of infinity built into the grammar. An infinite grammar! What could be more monstrous, or sublime? That's Spanish for you—it's like a baroque desert yeti, dragging you across an infinite plane: horizontal vertigo, forever. If you stop to consider it, you'll see how horrifyingly vertiginous Spanish can be. Do you follow me? I'm showing you Spanish in her underwear . . . This is just a glimpse of the contours of her most intimate bits, okay? And her lady parts are so luxurious, so voluptuous . . . they actually cause me pain."

Mona peered at Sven from behind her messy bangs. She wished she were wearing her contacts, but in spite of the blurry edges to everything, it seemed to her that, judging by his amused and alert smile, an object in Sven's mind called "Spanish" had begun to twist, to spiral into itself, taking on the new, unexpectedly hot shape she'd described. It was clear he liked listening to her.

"I guess my Spanish isn't sufficiently developed for me

to be able to see what you're describing," Sven remarked pensively.

A jubilant Lowena approached and handed them each a beer. When she spoke, it sounded like she was reciting email subject lines. Rather than a professional defect, this was, in fact, her superpower:

"Dear writers, on behalf of all of us who work for the Meeting, I salute you. On the occasion of this first victory of Sweden over the Rest of the World. A great day in the history of the Meeting! All I can say is: thank you!"

Mona and Sven held up their beer bottles to return Lowena's salute as she continued down the beach, handing out more beer to the losers. Everyone had relaxed; the other writers seemed to be enjoying themselves. At one end of the beach, Fabrizzio was still explaining to his Italian girlfriend, who'd flown in just for the Meeting, the tactics that had led to their ignominious defeat. Meanwhile, his co-captain devoted his energy to catching up on his beer intake. The rest of the Rest of the World had completely forgotten about the game.

"In Stockholm," Mona asked, "did you ever take Latin in school?"

"No, my school didn't offer Latin. It was for rich kids. My family didn't have that kind of money. But I remember wanting to study Latin."

"And how's your nonfiction coming along?"

"Well, I don't really know. I haven't written any. I don't consider what I do to be 'nonfiction'—I prefer writing novels. But I was a journalist for a while, and there was a time when I dabbled in literary criticism, but I realized that I'd lose all my friends if I kept at it, so . . . it was either stick to reporting the facts or move to another continent."

"There's always Nicaragua."

"In Costa Rica, living by the water, I might have been able to be a literary critic, sure. You hit the beach and read all day in a lounge chair, and then when the sun goes down you have a few beers and set the world to rights with a nasty review. Perfect."

"I don't know. Maybe you'd rather think about other things if you lived there. Maybe the rest of the world wouldn't matter to you that much anymore."

"But you have to keep flexing that muscle, don't you think? A friend of mine says that without hate, there is no art."

A long white cloud was cutting across the sky: the wake of a plane. The plane itself was too high to be seen.

About a hundred yards from where Mona sat with Sven, a slow and slight figure was now coming across the sand of the abandoned soccer field. It was Shingzwe. She was wearing an elegant wrap that fit right in with the sixties vibe at the lake; it fluttered in the breeze, allowing a view of her feet, moving like two silver-plated beetles. On her head was a mauve beret, which she secured with one hand, lest it fly off in the breeze coming in off the water. She crouched down in the sand, as if she were looking for something she'd lost. She did a lap around the beach, and, on her way back, passed by Mona and Sven with both her hands balled into fists.

"Good afternoon, Shingzwe," Sven called. "Were you looking for something you lost in the sand?"

Shingzwe stared without understanding. Sven pointed at her hands. Shingzwe brought her fists together and opened them to make a little bowl.

"Oh, I was looking for grains of sand, any that are still warm from the energy of the game, all the high spirits of competition. I wanted to take some home to my husband. When I tell him about the days I spent here, he'd be able to hold the sand and feel what it was like. Everyone had so much fun, didn't they? There was so much life in the game. So much beauty."

Without waiting for a response, Shingzwe sealed the bowl of her hands and said goodbye with a slight lift of her chin. Sven and Mona stared after her, bewitched, unable to contribute a single word to her statement. Could the life in letters be made that way, through the strength of incessant pacts with such details? Shingzwe's actions were as delicate as poems—like the poem about grains of rice and teacups she'd read that morning. Her simplicity shone as irrefutably as a diamond. She really knows what she's doing, Mona thought. What a pro. Then Mona remembered the way she totally lost it at lunch with Shingzwe, and was happy to find herself light-years away from the anguished feeling that had besieged her before that plateful of tears and moussaka . . .

"I'm not sure that hatred plays such an important role," Mona said at last. "But I do believe that contempt is the lingua franca of our era, and on that I'll bet we can both agree."

Sven wrapped his arms around his legs, his eyes roving the horizon. He was much handsomer up close than from far away—a rare quality. And proximity had bestowed yet another attractive quality on him: his voice exuded a warm sense of humor and a candid unpretentiousness.

"Now you're making me doubt myself. Because I don't know if I'm such a good hater. What I mean is that I don't think I'd be able to make much art from it. Any art that came out of my hatred would end up a failure. I'd just make myself miserable, and to no purpose. But I do think finding things to hate is an inevitable pastime, and when it comes to anything inevitable, the best you can do is enjoy it, maybe even sublimate it, as they say. Don't you think?"

Mona watched a front of cumulonimbus clouds assemble a fringe along the washed-out blue sky; this was surely the source of that chalky, dusty quality of the Swedish sun.

She said, "I was thinking recently that the history of ideas has also got to be the history of people liking each other. I mean, it's obvious, right? Art is marked by these moments when certain artists take a liking to each other. They get along, they become friends. Something like love circulates between them. This way of getting along and making friends and forming groups is then what we call, after a few decades have gone by, an avant-garde or a movement or the Boom or whatever. But the reason it all happens is just because once upon a time some people enjoyed being around certain other people, getting drunk and admiring each other, and they're all inspired by being so alike, whether they're writers or musicians or whatever. Without those moments when living, breathing people learn to appreciate other living, breathing people, without that love, there would be no avant-gardes . . . and our avant-gardes are like giant barges carrying rare, special works of art. Without those big avant-garde barges, the canals and rivers and waterways of art would get blocked up, or forgotten—there'd be no way to navigate them, and we would never be able to explore the limits of the collective imagination."

The clouds continued to advance, piling up against each other like a many-headed beast.

"So it's important to enjoy each other," Mona said. "And treat each other well. Love each other. Because that way you won't be the one to obstruct the emergence of a new vanguard just because somebody made a bad first impression, or because you don't like what someone else posted on Facebook. You don't want to be the Mark David Chapman of your generation's fetal avant-garde. Without love, without this glue to hold things together, there is no avant-garde, no movements. Only the fantasy of a community, or the feeling that we're privileged to share some crazy idyll—only that can save us."

"I like where you're going with this. Otherwise literary culture is nothing but a bunch of snipers scattered all over the world, each on their own rooftop, lining up their enemies in crosshairs of arguments and posturing . . ."

Mona shifted to lie on her side, drawing in the sand with her finger, letting the thick grains drag through her fingers.

"But there's some truth to what you said about hate. It makes things more legible. A black stone over a white stone, like in that César Vallejo poem, right? Hate makes a lot of groups visible, and makes certain discourses legible. Hate is ancient, yet when it bubbles to the surface it's as if an expedition of explorers hiking through a forest at night discovers a phosphorescent snake slithering across the ground, and suddenly nothing in the world is ever the same again, since now we know there's such a thing as fluorescent snakes. Actually we're the forest . . . the snake is slithering through *us*. But I don't know if we're really looking for that kind of legibility when we write. On the contrary: we write to try and get rid of the hate-colored glasses that make the world so stark and supposedly legible. Even when something becomes apparent and we're able to wrap our minds around it—maybe we don't want to tell everyone about it, don't want to rely on the codes in force, or use old words for new things. Maybe instead we just want to follow the snake back to its lair. Maybe we write to get down that hole, and figure out what's there, and come up with new words for it . . . Most people go through life trying to avoid that dark energy, and the mind trains itself to escape."

Mona's last phrase was left floating in the air. She'd spoken without thinking, improvising, letting herself wind up wherever the words led her. She let her head fall back on the ground, her dark hair spilling across the coarse sand. She put on her thick-framed glasses and closed her eyes.

Sven lay down beside her, his arm making two sides of

a triangle to prop up his head. Beyond the profile of Mona's face, the fjord dissolved into the blue haze.

"While you were talking, I was thinking . . . whatever distance we can put between ourselves and hatred? That's freedom—that's all the freedom we're likely to get. The bohemian lifestyle is this secular but sacred fantasy, right? When writers write, they aren't worrying about sustaining the culture . . . What they care about is finding that freedom, so their gift to the species—if you allow me—is their will to sustain that dream of bohemia. Writing is the only desire you can fully realize by yourself, alone with your mind. That's why there will always be writers. Our credo is that life can be a book, that it can be read and accessed by someone else. And writers are the evidence that life *is* a book, that it's written. Writers try to do something with what for the rest of humanity is just air."

Sven took a swig of his beer, his blue eyes reflecting the color of the sea. "Let's say that right now a Norse god emerges from the water and offers to grant you one wish. Would you wish for more love in your generation? Or for the secret sauce for getting down in that hole? What's the one thing you'd ask for tonight?"

"This night in particular?" Mona laughed, her hair extending like a black halo over the sand. She breathed in the bay air. "I'd like to know the private life of my unconscious thoughts," she said, more or less to herself.

Sven inched closer: he hadn't heard what she said.

"I'd like to see how the night ends."

Sven leaned his head forward, still resting it on the triangle of his arm. Mona looked at him askance, giving him side-eye by accident, appearing almost cross-eyed, and exhaled, her mouth shaped into a kiss.

Back in his cabin, Mona let herself fall into bed while Sven tugged at her leggings. The blinds were low, barely allowing a few thick tongues of the interminable white night into the room. Mona crawled toward the headboard and took off her blouse without unbuttoning it. The blue shadows enveloped her. Confident, in just her underwear, she arched her back against the firm bed, raising her waist like a little bridge. She held out her hand, inviting him to join her.

Sven remained beside the bed, immobile. Then he went away and came back. He was holding an electric lantern made to look like a kerosene lamp, similar to the one in Mona's cabin.

"Tell me what happened, Mona," he said.

And now, not content with the light of the lantern, Sven decided to kill the mood completely, and flipped on the overhead light.

"What happened? You have to tell me."

Mona sighed. She'd figured the light in the bedroom would be sufficiently low. It was easier on Skype. Real-life bedrooms are where the trouble starts.

"It's not okay, Mona. Who did that to you?"

Mona looked down at her body like someone standing at the edge of a cliff. How long did bruises last? Long enough. Under the cold overhead lights, the spectacle was all the more astonishing. Blue hematoma stains crossed her thighs, along with darker brown blotches that had begun to acquire yellow halos. She had cuts and bruises all over. Back in the sauna, the flickering lights had kept Lena from noticing— besides, Lena was too distracted to see anything besides her own caricature of Mona's appearance. And the only other person who'd been in the sauna, Akto Perksson, existed in his own Hellenic-Nordic world, where the bodies of women in a sauna were not to be decoded in a sexual way, and therefore barely registered at all.

"The thing is, I don't know. It's . . . confusing. All I know is I woke up like this." The colorless tone in which she said this somehow made the marks on her body seem all the more vivid.

"But who was with you at the time? You must remember who was there."

Mona watched the tungsten filament still quivering in the lantern. She wiped her face and shut her eyes, curling into a ball on the bed. In a thin thread of a voice, she said, "It's strange, but I have this memory that I died. I was dead. Only I don't remember the details."

Tears streamed down her cheekbones and past her dimples, reaching her lips, her chin. Sven kissed her. Mona's soft sobs gave way to a trembling. A strange, incongruent mirth.

"Your name. Sven Olle Siggurdsson. Your initials are S.O.S."

He just stood there, completely clothed, watching her. She reached out to him again. Instead of embracing her,

Sven took a swig of vodka and sat down on the bed to inspect Mona's wounds, his elbows on his knees. He watched her expression change into something cheerful and naughty under the tears. He tousled her hair and offered her a sip from his flask.

"There's only one day left here. Where are you going after that? You think you'll stay in Europe for a while? Please tell me you'll take care of yourself. That you'll be okay. Try to remember. You have to promise."

At last Sven lay down beside her. He placed his hand gently on her cheek, turning her face to his, and kissed her again. But the thing was, Mona *did* remember. Maybe not in the form of an intact memory, but rather as a series of images: A highway at night. Mojitos at the bar at Reposado, a Peruvian-Mexican fusion place in Palo Alto. Another round at La Bodeguita del Medio, a Cuban restaurant she really liked. Sitting there staring at her order of *ropa vieja*—and then a blank. Antonio, one of the guys in her program at Stanford, paying the bill. His car, his place, feeling the glass against her face, not being able to move because of the drugs. Ketamine, most likely, or Ambien. Sometimes Mona took Ambien to sleep, but recently it had also become a party drug. Inside Antonio's campus apartment, the light clicking off, murmurs and later screams. Unrecognizable screams, the screams of a woman, but she wasn't sure who. Seeing two dark backs, the backs of two men, a metallic bed frame. No sense of how much time had passed, or what had happened. Crossing the interminable campus. Sitting through class like a ghost. Waking up at Caltrain, her hair stuck to the ground. Seeing the alert on her phone, reminding her of the flight to Stockholm. Running her hands down her sticky body, numbed inside. The images shuffled like cards and continued to iterate in whatever order, because she didn't know what order was correct. All she felt was a deep knot under her lungs, in the center of her chest, an empty pain that she couldn't fill with words.

Sven was caressing her hair. The locks that touched her face were still wet. His face expressed a preemptive nostalgia. All this was about to disappear, and then the only thing left would be the memory of hair damp with the tears of a girl he'd just met.

He entered her gently, with painstaking care that Mona soon intensified, moving under him, kissing him without restraint, letting herself be carried away by the feeling of him inside her—a violence that made her feel lighter and lighter, like she was being hoisted on a mast, rocked by a storm.

10.

The long gray overcoat reached to his ankles, contributing to his priestly air. His somber expression contrasted with the idyllic landscape of a little port on the Swedish fjord. The dervish beard, thick and wild down to the center of his chest, indicated that his duties were not entirely of this world. Ragnar Tertius, the Icelandic poet, had at last made his much-anticipated appearance.

The organizers had set up a small podium on the beach so that the speaker would have his back to the lake. After his presentation would come the long-awaited climax, when the winner of the Basske-Wortz would be announced, and all the anticipation and intrigue of the Meeting would at last be dispelled. Arrayed before Ragnar were rows of white chairs brought down from the resort, making up an open-air auditorium in which everyone felt their hearts beating heavily in their chests, as if they were witnessing history in the making. Ragnar Tertius, the seer from the frozen northern seas, would first give one of his very rare public talks, with the Swedish dusk as his backdrop. Following his remarks, one of the invited guests would step up to receive the award: a small iron and glass statuette in the likeness of Havsrå, a sea creature from Swedish folklore. And, of course, a fat check.

The guests took their places just minutes before Ragnar Tertius appeared. The evening was cooler than the previous ones, and the writers had donned their finest. Hava's suitcase had finally been reunited with its owner, who was dressed in a long tunic coated in black and blue sequins. Abdollah was dashing in a blue suit with English tailoring, while Carmina flaunted another low-cut red dress. The Latvian poet had crowned his suit of carefully disheveled rags with a small top hat. Gemma was wearing a little blush dress and a leather jacket, while Marco, seated beside her, had added a large feather to his pirate getup. The event would be televised live, and everyone wanted to be presentable for the occasion— and for a potential triumphant walk to the podium.

Mona detected a few unfamiliar faces, probably reporters from Stockholm who'd been invited just for the prize ceremony. The two interpreters, from Icelandic to Swedish and from Icelandic to English, took their seats in a small gazebo immediately behind the audience. Two men in black placed the Havsrå statuette at the center of the podium, where everyone could see it.

The Icelandic poet ambled along the lakeshore. Slowly as he moved, there was something agile and athletic to his stride. It wasn't the gait of an elderly person. Indeed, his age seemed completely indeterminate. Perfectly contained in his own world, at no time did he make eye contact with any member of the audience that awaited him so eagerly. He mounted the steps to the podium and for a few moments stood in silence. His eyes were a frozen blue, ice floes in the Arctic night. His expression was extremely serious, disinterested in the outside world. He stared back at his audience as though he had no idea why they were there.

Ragnar let his gaze roam across the lake and then back up the hill that rose in undulations of wild grass up to the white tent. For an instant his eyes appeared to fix on a distant point, somewhere at the tops of the trees that surrounded the resort. Then he blinked, his gaze returning to the loudspeakers set up on the sand, the soccer goalposts, the little beachside bar. He could easily have been standing before a tank of rare, captive lizards, staring at them with the same intensity and lack of recognition.

It was like the Kafka story, but in reverse. In Kafka's tale, a literate monkey submits a report to an academy. But in this case it was them, the audience, who were the animals reporting to an authority: the Icelandic poet, who scrutinized them from his indomitable, icy perch. They were at his command.

Ragnar began by describing a blue plain, a flattened seascape. He said that moving among the dead always comes with a price. Orpheus not only descends to the kingdom of the dead; he's condemned to continue singing even after death. His quest to reclaim his beloved is a mere detail, a trick, a means of tracing the trajectory between one world and the other—yes, Eurydice is just a gimmick. *Writing is a mystical act*, Ragnar declaimed. *It traffics in energy. It is a dialogue with monsters. It conjures the state of limbo between the living and the dead.* In one version of the Orpheus myth, the Bacchae tear him limb from limb; in another version, nymphs find his head detached from his body, floating in the sea. They recognize him by his voice, even though by this point Orpheus is little more than a mutilated skull drifting on the current, singing an insane song whose lyrics are just a name, her name, the name of one who'd crossed to the other world.

Distracted by a rustling noise behind her, Mona turned around: it had seemed that the aura of attention that Ragnar produced was absolute, but in the meantime, something had changed. That sinister group of blond men dressed in black had occupied the back row. Now they, too, were listening in silence, eyes fixed on Ragnar.

The sky glowed purple over the mirrored lake, which multiplied the splendor of the evening light. The event had been perfectly synchronized to coincide with the sunset. Seated in the first row next to Lowena, Eino Eleino hung on Ragnar's every word. He was wearing white, as sharply dressed as Lowena, who was decked out in a mint-green silk pantsuit. It wasn't necessary to know the outcome for the event to be perfect, a splendid finale to Eino's tenure as director of the Meeting. He was preparing to enjoy the added prestige of getting to be the one to hand over the coveted Basske-Wortz Prize. When everything was finished, he'd confided to Lowena, he'd return to his cabin in the north of Sweden to finish a book of poems he was writing about

Emanuel Swedenborg. And after that, maybe he'd get back to the novel he'd started twenty years ago and never finished for lack of time . . . or because he never knew how to say goodbye to it, since part of him wanted to pursue it to the ends of the earth, as Orpheus had pursued Eurydice.

Strong purples and reds continued their dance in the firmament, and Ragnar's speech spiraled through digressions, generating a conceptual whirlwind through which he steadily advanced his construction: a sensational creature the likes of which none of them had ever seen.

Now he was saying that the coast of the North Sea sheltered rocky caves that once beheld the dark metaphysics of the Etruscan pirates, *whose white ships flew huge gold spiders or giant octopuses as their emblems.* The Etruscan pirates used their hawsers to tie living prisoners to the bodies of the dead. They interlaced them in such a way that the arms, legs, and eyes of each body were precisely aligned, the living mouths barely brushing the cadavers' lips in a perverse and lethal kiss. Then the pirates would wait and watch at some distance from the caves. The prisoners condemned to this fate would scream in horror, their cries invading every corner of the bay. They would gaze with hope at the birds of prey their prone bodies attracted, animals unconcerned with their screaming, masters of the virtue of patience. The prisoners tried to entice the birds closer, imagining that their pecking beaks might cut the ropes and free them. Later they understood that the birds would only come nearer when the nauseating stench of advanced putrefaction became irresistibly tempting, by which point they'd be as dead as the bodies to which they'd been tethered.

The process fascinated the ancients because it allowed them to witness the workings of death in slow motion. They watched the explosive transmutation of the body's palette: reds and yellows followed by tones of violet and black, a web of veins throbbing blue amid the swamp of streaks across the skin, drawing strange landscapes in the colors of death. And to prolong this erudite aesthetic pleasure, the Etruscans would continue taking food and water to the bound prisoners over the course of several days—serving, of course, only those of their guests who remained alive, those who still had a sustaining relationship to food, those who had not yet completed their own deaths, those who had not yet themselves become food.

Authors who are stuck in the past, who wish to sup upon it, to drain dry those pigments that blossom on the mouths of the dead, said Ragnar, they ought to be quite familiar with this methodology. They know they imitate a ghost their readers might be able, perhaps, to keep with them if they make their deaths an irresistible fact, like this explosion of colors in the night sky. They watch, these writers, as the Etruscans did before them, for a green stain to grow on their abdomens, one that expands as it swells; for the truce between hard and soft to come undone as their joints are encrusted with blue; and then for the final darkness, the black night that devours all.

They love to watch the transfer of this horrible thing

from one person to the next. They've chosen death as the medium of their secret communications—the transmission of one state to another. Their theory of reading is, therefore, a theory of death, death by contagion, the death that liquefies and spreads and silences the territory it conquers. Death is to them a form of language, a way of painting colors, and giving meaning to our bodies.

As Ragnar spoke, a layer of fog began to form over the lake. The fabulous tonalities of the sunset began to disperse, leaving the horizon a deep shade of blue that contrasted sharply with the white fog over the bay. The breeze intensified. Mona buttoned her raincoat, burying her nose in its upturned lapels. Sheathed in an elegant blue jacket, Chrystos cinched his dark green foulard. And behind them now, the band of mysterious blonds was gone. When she glanced back to be sure, it looked like they'd left something behind, lying across one of the seats. A staff. How could they have forgotten something like that?

Frozen in place, she watched as the other writers fidgeted uncomfortably in their chairs. Mona was sure she'd felt the ground shaking. Were earthquakes even possible here? The program assistants were staring at each other, incredulous. But Ragnar was unperturbed and continued reading in his deep voice, absorbed in his words, as though nothing in the world could silence or even distract him.

Darkness would quicken over the body of the living prisoner, he went on, and the Etruscans would continue to feed him, so as not to interfere with the sacred phases of this so-very-picturesque communion between the living and the dead. Eventually, some larvae would burrow out and open a passage between the two bodies, in the abdominal region, impregnating the living prisoner with hordes of diminutive intruders. And when the screaming was finally done, when both bodies went black, the work of art was considered to be complete, and the Etruscans, of course, ceased carrying food to the prisoner.

When they were accused of being monsters, by way of Roman propaganda that sought to discredit the union of Etruria and Carthage, the Etruscans made a reply, about which Saint Augustine would later write: The body, *soma*, is also a tomb, *sema*. The Etruscans believed that the human condition was to be tied to a body as it rotted; this was the only and most basic truth of life, and therefore, the only possible philosophy. Far from content with the mere formulation of this theory, the Etruscans were inspired to set it to work and see it in action: a metaphysics that functioned also as aesthetics. As both the theorists and agents of this motion-image of death, the Etruscans and their civilization dissolved into the map of Latium.

The lake behind Ragnar was churning. The blue line of the horizon was gone, hidden behind the mantle of fog, which had turned menacing and dark, nearly black, as though a wall of water had risen from the lake. The program assistants exchanged fascinated looks. Some watched the activity on the horizon while others turned to see the spectacle unfolding behind them, on the hills. Then a deafening rumble arose from the depths of the lake, and the entire bay acted as a sort of echo chamber, with the roar rising and reverberating between the hills and water.

Just then Mona's entire body shuddered at the sound of something alien to the scene. A cell phone was ringing. Still paralyzed with fear, Mona's eyes darted around until she recognized the sound of her own ringtone. Her phone was on silent, so it must have registered as an emergency call. It was a U.S. phone number.

"I'm watching you."

Mona looked over her shoulder, and all the terror she'd felt before returned in a surge of hatred. There was a man there, dressed in black, one she hadn't seen before. And it was him. She knew it. Why hadn't she realized it before? Mona ducked back down between the raised flaps of her raincoat. He'd been here the entire time. He was the one who left those terrible clues for her to find. Or had she really taken leave of her senses? She stared at the Icelandic poet and then glanced around at the choir of authors who had gathered to listen and to participate, without realizing it, in her own personal apocalypse.

Ragnar was still lecturing, though even his powerful voice was barely audible amid the deafening sounds emerging from the water. *All their work is vanity, the vanity of thinking the world can be changed with words, even destroyed by words alone.* Mona was both fascinated and terrified because she could see that everyone was as baffled as she was. No one seemed to understand what was happening, because she saw lines of worry draw themselves into the impassive faces of everyone present—her hosts, the Swedes, the Arabs. Hava, for one, had beaten a retreat, making her way back up the hill that led to Patrick Hus, carrying her white chair above her head. The lake water was rising, threatening to topple the podium. And the man in black had vanished.

We've entered the forbidden laboratories that define what can be communicated from one person to another. But here, I see nothing more than vanity. You have all betrayed your pact with the dead. Disoriented, the writers were chattering among themselves one moment, taking pictures with their phones the next, or else trying to find some explanation for these phenomena, whatever they were, on the internet. Was the man in black hiding? Or right behind her, too close for her to see him, just out of the range of her peripheral vision? She still allowed for the possibility that she had hallucinated him. That he was flickering in and out of view like some devastating hologram.

Ragnar's speech had evolved or devolved into a language incomprehensible to all present, save perhaps the interpreters, who didn't even bother to keep up after the sound system shorted out. Ragnar stared down the program assistants as he spoke, as though he knew everything about them, more than they knew about themselves—as though he could see right through their clothes and the chairs some of them now cowered behind. He raised his hands high above his head as he recited a poem in ancient Icelandic.

Which was when a wall of water really did rise from the

lake, pricking everyone below it with preliminary droplets as it crashed first against Ragnar's back, his arms still held aloft, eyes lost somewhere in the hills beyond. In the surge of water, the iron and glass Havsrå statuette, the physical embodiment of the Basske-Wortz Prize, fell to the ground, caressed by the receding wave. The earth shook once more, the waters trembled, and the colors of the sky were obliterated by dense indigos, almost black. The storm unleashed fury in the sky, and night seethed over the lake in a gust of darkness.

Behind Ragnar, a mass began to swell in the center of the lake. It looked like a squall from the high seas, a column of water elevating over the gray plane, diffuse in the distance. The director of the festival watched, openmouthed. He took Lowena by the shoulder as she raised her hand, still holding a folder, waving for the writers to take refuge in the beachside café. Through the turmoil of the lake they glimpsed a hideous shape. The hindquarters of some prodigious animal.

It was something new. Something no one had ever seen before, emerging like a second storm from the frothy waters of the bay. At last the writers flew into a panic and fled. Amid the screams and toppling chairs, Mona spotted Lena Bactreau, still in her seat, eyes closed, moving her lips like she was saying a prayer.

It looked like a serpent of colossal dimensions, pocked by brilliant scales, but with something even more monstrous about it than its shape—it possessed something like a human expression.

Ragnar was repeating a name: Jörmungandr, Jörmungandr.

171

The earth seemed to respond with a tremor that echoed the name: Jörmungandr, Jörmungandr. *Jörmungandr will drag himself from the sea and poison the skies. His jaws will drip with venom and he will slither between the fire and the feet of giants.* Jörmungandr would guide them through a system of endless caves beneath the seas. When a ray of sunlight struck him, his victims would be able to see, for the last time, the eyes of the dead trapped beneath his translucent scales.

Could this serpent be the embodiment of all the literature of the infinite past? As part of her studies in Amazonian culture, Mona had explored the aquarian mythologies of many other latitudes, and was familiar with the name: Jörmungandr was a Norse mythological sea serpent with a beard of tentacles who lived at the bottom of the sea. Mona considered the death of art, the death of history, the death of the novel: fatalities that had progressed in succession since before the turn of the twentieth century. What would be the result if all those deaths could have had some sort of geological impact? If ideas produce physical force, the virulence of this inexplicable being could derive from all those deaths colliding against each other. Or, anyway, this was what she thought Ragnar might be trying to say . . . none of which could quite succeed in explaining the surreal spectacle of destruction she was now witnessing. She hugged herself, a ball of flesh and hair in her seat.

And then she remembered. She remembered that this was exactly how she'd remained, for hours, clasping her legs in shock, the tears streaming down her face after Antonio, her fellow Stanford doctoral candidate—following a drinking binge with certain additives back at his student-housing apartment—had punched her in the neck and kicked her as she lay on the floor, unable to resist, for minutes that felt like hours, and all because of a strange argument they'd gotten into while they were having sex, sex that became strange and painful, during which she asked him to stop, but he seemed not to hear her until Mona jumped up and tried to make it to the door, to escape in the nude, but he caught her by the foot and then, stepping on her ankle with his boot so she couldn't get away, brought the entire contents of his bookcase down on top of her—it was the closest thing to hand—hurling tomes of political economy off the shelves and onto Mona, who howled in fear as she felt pounds of paper battering her naked body. And her cries drove Antonio totally out of his mind because, as he later explained in various messages that Mona never answered, it had been an accident, he never would have wanted his precious library to come crashing down on a naked girl, much less her, he liked her a lot and she was so pretty. But her scream, that crazed and guttural scream, like some fucking shrill Latin American bitch—it annoyed him so much that in a fit of rage he'd jumped on top of her, kicking and stomping her as she lay there under his library. And since she wouldn't shut up, he dragged her by the hair into the bathroom and pushed her into the shower so he could wash off any sign that he'd been near or inside that body—not to protect himself, he explained, while he scrubbed soap across her skin and shampoo through her hair, sticking fingers dripping with antibacterial soap into her vagina—he was doing it to protect her from causing a problem it was best not to think about, a problem it was better not to get into, best not to even consider, like for example if she talked to anybody from university services, because they'd eventually suspend her visa, since nobody would believe her.

And while she was in the shower, shocked and numbed by the blows, half her body covered in suds, she looked so good, he told her, that he'd had to try to kiss her several times, to kiss and make up and finish in the shower what they'd started in the bed, since things in bed had been going so well, and how since she wouldn't kiss him back, since she was staring at him totally vacant, like she'd fainted, but she hadn't fainted, and Antonio didn't know, he couldn't know, if she was pretending—Are you pretending, Mona?—he gave her a big hug, and he started crying, too, and he told her that he'd been so frightened when he heard that scream rattle out of her as he wrapped his arms around her there in the shower, why was she screaming when they could whisper? Why are you screaming, he'd screamed in her ear, at the distance of a whisper, there's no reason to scream, he'd told her as he smashed her head against the bathroom tiles, after which Mona completely lost track of what happened, lying there beneath the water still raining over her.

Somehow Antonio had gotten her to the Caltrain platform, a place where she often went anyway, and she'd come to without a clear sense of how she'd gotten there. But now the memory and the humiliation returned with such force that she saw it all again, Antonio's face whispering threats in her ear, cursing her, hitting her, smiling, caressing her sticky wet hair, trying to wash it out as she sat there unconscious, because she was unconscious, but she could still see him in the mirror, like she was the proverbial fly on the wall, or rather as if the bathroom light had become some kind of omniscient third eye, since she saw it all from above: Antonio kissing her, thinking she was unconscious, Antonio touching her, caressing her neck and legs, reaching for the fur on her pelvis before she bit off a piece of his lip. And then the last slap, so hard that it threw her back against the metal shower knobs. And now she thought: It wasn't just that time. There were many others, and she'd kept going, blinded by an awful fascination for which she had no name.

And then, nothing. Maybe he thought she was dead. Maybe she thought she was dead, too. Or not completely dead. Only a part of her had died there, and that was why, for a few moments, she didn't care that the end of the world was unfolding at a Nordic waterfront retreat. If nothing else, the sky, with its storm, its muted and swirling colors, was majestic—as though reality had always been waiting there for her, up in the clouds, where only gods could play at art.

She felt a hand on her shoulder. Then her arm. It was Sven. Together they ran along the shore, toward the woods adjacent to the beach. The ground opened beneath them, and as the lake rose over their bodies in another wall of water, Jörmungandr dived back into the depths between columns of black foam. The glorious sky shattered overhead, and the beachside café was engulfed by a mudslide that came down the hills, devouring everything in its path. Mona watched as Abdollah's orange glasses floated by. Farther away, among the chairs, Carmina's red heels were sinking into the water. Chrystos's foulard flew across the beach and disappeared, swallowed by a turbulent waterspout rising from the water. Lena Bactreau was howling at the sky, but mute, her face contorted, as though she wished to face the end head-on, and with an argument on her lips. Akto wore a fascinated, fairly calm expression when the waters came for him. Philippe threw himself into a wave as it crashed in a conflagration of black, purple, and blue. Ragnar's dark visage, and his hands, elevated over the world, were nowhere to be seen.

The writers who'd made it up the hills found the ground closing over them like a carnivorous flower, having allowed them to alight on its soft undulations only to devour them. In the distance, Patrick Hus crumbled in silence, sucked down by an implacable force, falling like a house of cards while the white tent came untethered and flew into the storm, as if it had never known anything but the rain and the dust and the nothing.

ACKNOWLEDGMENTS

I wish to thank Emiliano Kargieman, Victoria Liendo, Maxine Swann, Ana Pérez and Gonzalo Garcés, my translator Adam Morris, and all the writers I've met and who have greeted me with their friendship and theatrics through the years.

A NOTE ABOUT THE AUTHOR

Pola Oloixarac was born in Buenos Aires in 1977. Her debut novel, *Savage Theories*, was a breakout bestseller in Argentina and was nominated for the Best Translated Book Award, and in 2010, *Granta* recognized her as one of the best young Spanish-language novelists. She was awarded the 2021 Eccles Centre & Hay Festival Writer's Award. Oloixarac is a regular contributor to *The New York Times*, the BBC, and *Rolling Stone*, and her fiction has appeared in *Granta*, *n+1*, *The White Review*, and an issue of *Freeman's* on "The Future of New Writing." Previously a resident of San Francisco, California, she currently resides in Barcelona.

A NOTE ABOUT THE TRANSLATOR

Adam Morris has translated novels by Beatriz Bracher, João Gilberto Noll, and Hilda Hilst. He is the author of *American Messiahs: False Prophets of a Damned Nation*.